P9-DBO-753

Full-Court Press

the
JOY
of
READING
Dedicated to the memory
of Hale Joy, 1995

This book belongs to:

HAPPY HOLIDAYS

The Ellsworth American.
Downtown Ellsworth

and

Mount Desert **Islander**
Downtown Bar Harbor

Also by Elena Delle Donne

My Shot

Hoops

Elle of the Ball
Full-Court Press
Out of Bounds

2

Elena Delle Donne

Simon & Schuster Books for Young Readers
New York London Toronto Sydney New Delhi

If you purchased this book without a cover, you should be aware that this book is stolen property. It was reported as "unsold and destroyed" to the publisher, and neither the author nor the publisher has received any payment for this "stripped book."

SIMON & SCHUSTER BOOKS FOR YOUNG READERS
An imprint of Simon & Schuster Children's Publishing Division
1230 Avenue of the Americas, New York, New York 10020
This book is a work of fiction. Any references to historical events, real people, or real places are used fictitiously. Other names, characters, places, and events are products of the author's imagination, and any resemblance to actual events or places or persons, living or dead, is entirely coincidental.
Text copyright © 2018 by Elena Delle Donne
Cover illustrations copyright © 2018 by Cassey Kuo
All rights reserved, including the right of reproduction in whole or in part in any form.
SIMON & SCHUSTER BOOKS FOR YOUNG READERS is a trademark of Simon & Schuster, Inc.
For information about special discounts for bulk purchases, please contact Simon & Schuster Special Sales at 1-866-506-1949 or business@simonandschuster.com.
The Simon & Schuster Speakers Bureau can bring authors to your live event. For more information or to book an event, contact the Simon & Schuster Speakers Bureau at 1-866-248-3049 or visit our website at www.simonspeakers.com.
Also available in a Simon & Schuster Books for Young Readers hardcover edition
Cover design by Laurent Linn
Interior design by Hilary Zaryky
The text for this book was set in Minister.
Manufactured in the United States of America
0519 OFF
First Simon & Schuster Books for Young Readers paperback edition June 2019
2 4 6 8 10 9 7 5 3 1
The Library of Congress has cataloged the hardcover edition as follows:
Names: Delle Donne, Elena, author.
Title: Full-court press / Elena Delle Donne.
Description: First edition. | New York : Simon & Schuster Books for Young Readers, [2018] | Series: Hoops ; 2 | Summary: When Elle begins to volunteer two days a week working with children with special needs, she has trouble juggling her new passion, basketball obligations, and schoolwork.
Identifiers: LCCN 2017051752 | ISBN 9781534412347 (hardback) | ISBN 9781534412354 (pbk) ISBN 9781534412361 (eBook)
Subjects: | CYAC: Basketball—Fiction. | People with disabilities—Fiction. | Voluntarism—Fiction. | Middle schools—Fiction. | Schools—Fiction. | BISAC: JUVENILE FICTION / Sports & Recreation / Basketball. | JUVENILE FICTION / Girls & Women. | JUVENILE FICTION / Social Issues / Self-Esteem & Self-Reliance.
Classification: LCC PZ7.1.D64814 Ful 2018 | DDC [Fic]—dc23
LC record available at https://lccn.loc.gov/2017051752

For my goddaughter, Gia,
and all the young ballers out there

Acknowledgments

I have a team of people that I would like to thank, and I fully recognize that I would not be where I am today without the support of my family and friends behind me.

Amanda, my wife and my best friend, you have given up and sacrificed so much to help me better my career (even being my off-season workout partner). Words cannot express how much you mean to me, and I am so excited that you are with me for life. We are a pretty unstoppable team.

Special thanks to my incredible parents, who have been with me since day one. Mom, thank you for being extremely honest, absolutely hilarious, and my ultimate role model for what strength looks like.

Dad, thank you for driving me all the way to Pennsylvania twice a week, attending every AAU tournament, and still traveling to lots of my WNBA games. You are my biggest fan.

To my older sister, Lizzie, thank you for helping me keep everything in perspective. You remind me that there is so much more to life, and that joys can come from anywhere—even something as simple as the wind or a perfectly cooked rib eye. You are the greatest gift to our family. And thanks to my big brother, Gene, for being able to make me laugh, especially through the lows, and for being my biggest cheerleader.

Wrigley, my greatest friend and Greatest Dane. Thanks for being my rock in Chicago and for attacking me with love every time I come home. Rasta, thanks for being the edge and sass in our home and for being the only one in our house who can keep Amanda in check.

Erin Kane and Alyssa Romano, thank you for helping me discover myself and for helping me find my voice. This wouldn't have happened without the greatest team behind me.

Thanks to my Octagon literary agent, Jennifer Keene, for all her great work on this project. Thanks to the all-stars at Simon & Schuster, including Liz Kossnar.

Thank you all.

Bad Dog, Good Dog!

My dog, Zobe, had been mine for only twenty-four hours, and he was already part of our family.

My parents had surprised me the day before by driving me and my older brother, Jim, to the animal shelter to adopt him. I'd seen Zobe at an adoption event at the mall and had fallen in love with him. He was a big Great Dane, sweet and goofy, and bigger than all of the other dogs. Kind of like me.

I mean, of course I'm bigger than the other dogs. But at six feet tall, I'm also bigger than everyone else in the seventh grade. And I hadn't been having an easy time of it. Zobe was bigger than the other dogs, and he was adorable. So it made me think that being awkwardly big wasn't the worst thing ever.

Zobe's tail was wagging like crazy when we brought him home. He went from room to room, sniffing the floor. When he got to my sister Beth's room, he bounded up to her wheelchair.

It had worried me for a minute. Beth was born deaf and blind, and I thought Zobe might startle her. But her hand had reached out and touched his fur, and she smiled.

"We let Beth in on the surprise," Mom had explained. "She knew Zobe was coming."

After that, Zobe had run upstairs. Mom and Dad had said that Zobe could sleep in my room, so I scrambled after him with the dog bed we'd just bought at the pet supply shop. But Zobe hadn't been interested in the dog bed. He'd jumped into mine, and that's where he'd stayed all night.

I'd woken up pretty tired this morning, and it wasn't just because it's hard for a Great Dane and a six-foot-tall human to share a twin-size bed. I'd also stayed up late researching Great Danes, so I could be a good owner for Zobe.

One of the things I'd learned was that Great Danes need thirty to sixty minutes of exercise a day, so I'd put Zobe on his leash and headed to Greenmont Park with him right after school. My friend Blake came with me, and I started telling him all the Great Dane facts I'd learned.

"So, Zobe's coloring is called blue," I was saying, as we made our way along the circular walking path.

"Blue?" Blake repeated. "He looks kind of gray."

"Great Danes can be different shades of gray, but they're called blue," I explained. "Dogs with shiny gray fur are called steel blue. I think Zobe is more of a slate blue. What do you think?"

Blake nodded. "That makes sense," he said.

"And he's supposed to eat three or four small meals a day, instead of one big one," I went on, "or he could get sick."

Blake looked Zobe up and down. "I bet he needs a lot of food."

"He does," I said. "I can feed him in the morning and at night, and Mom says she'll feed him during the day."

A woman came walking toward us with a tiny white Chihuahua on a pink leash. I made sure I had both hands on Zobe's leash.

"The animal shelter said that Zobe is good with other dogs, but I still need to be careful," I explained to Blake.

"Definitely," he agreed. "Zobe could eat that dog up for a midnight snack!"

When we were about three feet away from the Chihuahua, the little dog started to yap loudly. Zobe's tail started to wag. He lurched ahead of me, pulling me with him. Then he stopped short in front of the Chihuahua and started sniffing her. The little dog quieted down.

"That's a beautiful dog you've got there," the woman said, smiling at us.

"Thanks," I replied. "His name is Zobe."

She gave a little tug on the Chihuahua's leash. "Come on, Tink, let's say good-bye to Zobe."

Tink's tail was wagging too as they headed away, and I gave Zobe a pat.

"Good boy, Zobe," I said.

We were nearing the fenced-in dog park, where dog owners could let their pets off leash to run around freely. I scanned it, hoping to see my friend Amanda there. Which, I have to admit, is another reason why I had rushed to walk Zobe after school. I get really happy whenever I run into Amanda. But Amanda and her dog, Freckles, an English springer spaniel, were not there.

"Are you going to let Zobe run around in the dog park?" Blake asked.

I stopped and studied the park. Two miniature poodles were chasing each other while a mom and twin toddlers looked on. One adorable, medium-size mutt with brown shaggy fur was playing catch with his owner, a guy wearing a University of Delaware T-shirt.

"I think he'll be fine," I said.

We entered the dog park and closed the gate behind us. I let Zobe off his leash with a click.

He took off like a rocket! I thought he was going to go after one of the dogs, but instead he made a beeline for the toddlers. He started to lick the face of one, an adorable boy with curly black hair, and the sheer force of him sent the poor kid tumbling backward!

I lunged for Zobe.

"Zobe, no!" I yelled, and I grabbed his collar and pulled him away. Blake helped the little boy to his feet, and I turned to the mom. "I'm so sorry! Is he okay?"

To my relief, the little boy was laughing.

"Big doggie!" he said, and the mom looked at me with concern on her face.

"He's fine," she said. "But you might want to keep your dog on a leash until he's better trained."

"Of course!" I said, and I could feel my cheeks getting hot with embarrassment. I snapped the leash on Zobe's collar, nodded to Blake, and headed for the gate.

"Well, *that* was a bad idea," I said as we walked away. "I feel awful!"

"Aw, that kid loved it," Blake told me.

I frowned. "Maybe, but what if he had gotten hurt? I think I need obedience classes for Zobe."

Blake took out his phone and started typing and scrolling. "There's one dog training school here in Greenmont, and three in Wilmington. They train problem dogs, puppies, therapy dogs. . . ."

I sighed. "I don't think Zobe is a *problem* dog, is he? I mean, he can't help it if he loves people."

"I think he just needs regular training," Blake said. He patted Zobe's head. "Don't worry. He's a great dog."

"Thanks, Blake," I said, and we continued our walk around the park.

There's a reason why Blake and I are best friends, and it's not just because the Tanakas have lived next door to us since I was a baby. Blake is chill. He always knows the right thing to say. And he loves basketball as much as I do.

We looped around the park twice and then headed home. I didn't see Amanda at all, and I felt a twinge of disappointment. But it didn't last long. I knew I'd see her at school tomorrow, and at basketball practice that afternoon. And every Monday, Wednesday, Friday, and Sunday after that. During basketball season, our practice and game schedule got pretty intense.

When we got to our street, Carrie Lane, we came to Blake's house first. Mrs. Tanaka was pulling weeds in the beautiful flower garden on their front lawn. She stood up when she saw us.

"Elle, this must be the famous Zobe I've heard so much about!" she said, standing up.

I kept Zobe on the leash and walked toward her. He jumped up and placed his front paws on her shoulders.

"My, he's a big boy!" she said, laughing.

I pulled him off of Blake's mom. "Yes," I said. "I just need to teach him some manners. He's really friendly—maybe *too* friendly!"

Blake nodded to me. "Later," he said. "Gotta get on my science homework."

"Oh yeah, right," I said. I'd nearly forgotten about homework, because I'd been so Zobe-obsessed. "See you tomorrow!"

I walked to my house next door, and when I got inside I took Zobe off the leash. He bounded over to his water dish and started lapping like crazy, just as Mom wheeled in Beth.

I walked over to greet Beth with my usual hug. All the things I do with my eyes and ears, Beth does with smell, touch, and taste. When I hugged her, she sniffed the top of my head so she could tell it was me.

As I was hugging Beth, a big, doggy head squeezed in between us.

"Zobe, no!" I cried. But Beth started nodding her head up and down, and I knew that meant she was happy—she liked Zobe. Then she grabbed my hand and formed a symbol on it.

I didn't recognize what the symbol meant, and I looked at Mom.

"Did Beth learn a new symbol?" I asked.

Mom nodded. "We came up with a symbol for dog," she said. "Beth is very curious about Zobe, and when you were at school today he spent most of the day with her. He's such a sweetheart!"

I formed the "dog" symbol into Beth's hand, and she nodded her head again. Then I formed another symbol: *good*.

Yes, Beth replied, tracing on my palm.

"Elle, please wash up and help me get ready for dinner," Mom said.

"Sure," I said. When I came back from the bathroom, I saw that Zobe was sitting next to Beth with his head in her lap. She was nodding her head, and he had a look of blissful peace on his face.

"Wow!" I said. "They're both so happy!"

Mom nodded and handed me a bag of baby carrots. "Can you chop these up please?" she asked, and she glanced over at Beth and Zobe. "Zobe really is a great addition to the Deluca household. He's a wonderful dog."

"He is," I said. "But, um, something happened at the park today. . . ."

I told her about Zobe knocking down the little kid, and Mom frowned.

"Hmm," she said. "That is a problem. I guess Zobe can't go to the dog park until he's better trained."

"Yeah," I agreed. "Blake said maybe he could go to obedience school." And as I said the words, another thought hit me.

"Some of the obedience schools also train dogs to become therapy dogs!" I said, feeling excited at the thought. "Zobe is so good with Beth—he'd be a fantastic therapy dog."

I put down my carrot-chopping knife and grabbed my phone.

"Look, there's one right here in Greenmont!" I said.

Mom closed the oven door. "Elle, I'm not saying that getting some training for Zobe is a bad idea," she said. "But maybe training him to be a therapy dog right now is not the smartest thing. You're so busy with your schoolwork, and with basketball. When would you find the time?"

"It's only one day a week!" I protested. "I could fit it in."

Mom sighed. "I'll talk to your father about it, Elle. But I'm not making any promises. You have to trust us to know what's best for you sometimes."

I looked away from Mom and rolled my eyes. I get good grades, I keep my room (mostly) neat, and Mom is always telling Grandma and Grandpa what a "responsible young girl" I am. So why wasn't she trusting me with this? Zobe would make an awesome therapy dog, I just knew it.

I'd have to find some way to convince her, but I knew that it would take time.

Caught on Video

L ook alive, Elle!"

Dina Garcia tossed a basketball at me as I stepped into the gym the next day after school. I quickly caught it and then dribbled up to the basket and sank an easy layup.

"Nice job!" Dina said, and she held out a hand for me to slap it. Even though she's one of the shortest players on the team, Dina's got a ton of confidence.

I tossed the ball back to her, and she dribbled away. The rest of the team was warming up on the court, but there was no sign of Coach Ramirez yet.

Everyone was still feeling pretty pumped after winning our first game of the season on Sunday against the North Creek Chargers.

Well, mostly great. I had scored pretty well, but thanks to the fact that I have still not figured out how to control my extra-long legs, I'd made some mistakes and managed to get a few violations.

Avery Morgan, my other best friend, ran up to me in the gym.

"Hey, Elle!" she said, and then let out a breath. "Glad I'm not late. I had to stay late in French class to go over a quiz with Mademoiselle Bernard."

"Uh-oh," I said.

Avery shrugged. "Let's just say I did not do *très bien*. But I can retake the quiz if I go for extra help tomorrow." She shook her head. "Why didn't I just stick with Spanish? I was so good at that!"

"You'll get it, Avery," I said. "You're the smartest person I know."

Avery gently punched me in the shoulder. "Thanks, Elle!"

At that moment, Coach Ramirez came into the

gym, wheeling a TV set on a metal cart. She's super fit, and her dark brown hair is cut sporty and short.

"All right, I finally got this thing working," she said. "Before we get on the court today, we're going to watch some highlights of Sunday's game. Hannah's dad is going to be recording all of our games this season."

Some of the girls clapped, but not me. I was still having flashbacks of the mistakes I'd made. The last thing I needed was a video replay!

"It'll be okay, Elle," Avery whispered to me as we took our seats in the bleachers. I tried to smile at her. There's a reason why she's my other best friend. Just like Blake, she knows how I'm feeling without me having to say anything, and she's always able to calm me down.

Everyone quieted down as coach got the video going. Hannah's dad, Mr. Chambal, had started out the video by getting a shot of the players on the bench at the start of the game. There was Hannah next to her best friend, Natalie, and they were whispering to each other. Dina came next, anxiously bouncing her right leg up and down—you could tell she was dying to get into the game. Next to her was Caroline, who was smiling and waving at someone in the stands. And finally came Amanda, with her cute freckles and reddish-brown hair, cheering for the rest of us on the court.

Then the camera moved to the court. There I was in the center, towering over everybody. Avery was on my right, ready to get into position as point guard. Patrice Ramirez, the coach's daughter, was next to her, playing small forward.

Bianca Hidalgo and Tiff Kalifeh were on my left, focused and waiting for the ref to blow his whistle. Tiff, one of our strongest, most consistent players, wore a green-and-yellow hijab to match our Nighthawks uniforms. And Bianca, our shooting guard, was just as talented. Last year, I had played shooting guard, but Coach Ramirez moved me to center because of my height. Bianca, who loved playing center, hadn't been too happy about that.

The ref's whistle blew, and I sprang up to get the opening jump ball. I batted it to Patrice, and she hesitated before passing it to Bianca. The ref's whistle blew, and he yelled, "Back court violation!"

Coach Ramirez stopped the tape at this point.

"Did you see what Patrice did there?" she asked. "She hesitated! She froze! That's why we lost possession of the ball there. Everybody needs to be thinking on their feet out there, got it?"

"Got it!" we all shouted back, and I saw Patrice look down at her basketball shoes, her cheeks flushed pink. Coach was always harder on Patrice than the rest of us, probably because she was her daughter, I guessed. (Although that didn't explain why she was harder on me than most of the other players, as well.)

Coach fast-forwarded the tape and stopped at a point where I was jumping up to take a shot, but I ended up flat on my back with the ball still between my hands. One of the Chargers took the ball from me.

Coach stopped the tape. "What exactly happened there, Elle?"

I could feel my face get hot, and I wasn't exactly sure what to say. It was hard to explain that my body had sprouted up several inches over just a few months, and I didn't know how to work it—which was the truth, not an excuse. I felt like one of those mecha machines in a sci-fi movie—one of those giant robots with a human operating its movements from inside. My brain was the operator, and my body was the giant robot.

But I couldn't say that to Coach. Instead, I said, "Not sure, Coach."

"This tells me we need to do more footwork drills with you, Elle," Coach said.

She fast-forwarded again, and the next thing she stopped for was a flawless three-point shot that Avery sank.

"Nice form there, Avery," Coach said, and Avery beamed happily as Coach explained to everyone what Avery had done right.

Coach paused a few more times during the tape to show us some more positive stuff—from Bianca and Tiff, but not anyone else—and most of the moments she focused on were when we messed up. Except for me, Patrice got the worst of it. The player guarding her kept stealing the ball from her.

As for me, Coach focused on another stellar moment of mine: when I went leaping out of bounds. I had been charging down the court and couldn't control my speed. I cringed watching it. What a rookie mistake!

"Runaway train!" Bianca yelled when Coach showed us the clip, and some of the girls laughed.

"All right, simmer down," Coach Ramirez said, and then she looked at me. "But seriously, Elle, you've got to learn how to put the brakes on out there. You made some great shots, but those penalties are going to keep hurting us."

I nodded mutely. It felt pretty awful, being singled out more than once for mistakes I'd made, especially since I thought I'd done some good things in the game. I'd scored points, including a basket scored from a pretty awesome rebound. Why hadn't Coach mentioned that? Maybe it wasn't as awesome as I'd thought it was.

Coach ended the session with the last basket of the game, made by Bianca. Of course. She made it right after the Chargers center knocked the ball out of my hands. Bianca had recovered it to make the winning shot.

"Now that's what I like to see!" Coach said when she stopped the tape. "Bianca stayed focused, kept her cool, and made the best of a bad situation."

I glanced at Bianca, who looked like she was about to burst with pride. I couldn't blame her. She was a really excellent player, and she'd saved the game for us.

Coach turned off the TV. "We won that game, but it was close. *Too close*. We need to do better."

She clapped her hands. "All right, ten laps around the gym, and then we're gonna do some footwork drills!"

We finished our laps, and Coach got us started on the drills. I don't think I had ever done so many footwork drills in one session! It was pretty intense.

First, we each placed a basketball on the floor in front of us. Then we had to jump up and put our left foot on the ball, then our right foot, then our left . . . we did this while Coach counted to a hundred.

Then Coach brought out jump ropes, and we

had to use them to jump on one foot. Fifty reps on the left, fifty reps on the right, and then fifty more alternating each foot.

After that, she set up six cones along the center line, about six feet apart. We had to run down the line, and when we got to a cone, we had to circle around it backwards, and then move on to the next cone and do the same. When we reached the end of the line, we had to go back and do it again. I knocked down one of the cones, but Hannah and Patrice did too, so I didn't feel so bad.

We moved to another cone drill next. Coach set up one cone in the center of the court, with a cone at four points on either side of it—kind of like a cross with a dot in the middle. We had to start at one of the outer cones and run forward to the cone in the center. Then we had to shuffle sideways from the center cone to the next cone in the cross. Then back to the center cone, running forward. Then to the next cone, shuffling, until we were all the way around the court.

I didn't knock any cones over this time, but it was hard to remember to switch from moving forward to sideways, and Coach yelled, "Focus, Elle!" more than once during that drill.

Practice was almost over by the time we finished our drills, but we managed to fit in a short scrimmage—and although it was short, I managed to get a violation. I was dribbling toward the basket, and then I picked up the ball to make my shot. But I lost my balance and took three steps forward.

"Traveling!" Coach barked. "You're only allowed two steps, Elle! You know that!"

Of course I knew that. I knew every basketball rule inside and out. But just because my brain knew the rules didn't mean that my arms and legs obeyed them.

Before we could head to the locker room to get our stuff, Coach gathered us all together.

"Just a reminder that tomorrow is our service day," she said. "We'll be volunteering with the kids from Camp Cooperation—that's the after-school program for elementary school kids with special needs."

Avery frowned and raised her hand. "Coach, I'm supposed to get extra help from Mademoiselle Bernard tomorrow after school. Is that okay?"

Coach Ramirez nodded. "The service day isn't mandatory, but I hope most of you can make it. Does anyone else need to miss it?"

Tiff had a math team match, and Caroline had a dentist appointment, but everyone else said they could go. Coach dismissed us, and we went to get our backpacks from the locker room.

"I hope I can get out of my French lesson in time to help out with the kids," Avery remarked. "It sounds like fun."

"Although, honestly, I'm a little nervous," Hannah said. "I mean, don't we need special training? What if we do the wrong thing?"

"Or say the wrong thing?" Natalie added.

The four of us were walking through the school halls by now. I knew, from growing up with Beth, that sometimes people were nervous being around her for the same reasons.

"Don't be nervous," I said. "They're just kids. Just be nice to them and have fun, like you would with any other kid."

Avery nodded. "That makes sense."

"Well, I'm kind of excited for tomorrow," I said. "I mean, I know I'll be better at it than I was at practice today! For some reason, I am stinking at basketball this season."

"Don't be so hard on yourself, Elle," Avery said. "You scored more points than anybody at Sunday's game. Don't let Coach get you down."

"It's hard not to," I said. "She must be being tough on me for a reason. I'm just not that good anymore."

"Of course you are!" Avery protested, but the thought that I wasn't good at basketball anymore was bugging me.

I am a terrible dancer. When I sing in the shower, Jim always bangs on the door and tells me to stop. In art class I am most comfortable drawing stick figures.

But I've been good at basketball since third grade, when I started playing. I always felt confident that no matter what happened anywhere else, I'd do great on the court.

Now . . . now, I wasn't so sure.

Some Things I'm Actually Good At

Good morning on this beautiful Wednesday, Spring Meadow students!" Principal Lubin's voice came over the school PA system. "Today I'm wondering if anybody knows what happened to the plant in Mr. Johnson's math classroom? Because it looks like it's grown square roots!"

On the first day of school, everybody in class would have groaned. But it was late fall, and we'd already heard so many of Principal Lubin's corny jokes that nobody made the effort anymore.

Most of us had been listening to Principal Lubin's

jokes for years. That's because Spring Meadow is a private school in Wilmington, Delaware, that goes from kindergarten through twelfth grade. There are only about fifty kids in each grade, and the elementary school, middle school, and high school kids each have their own building, but we all share the same principal.

He led us in the Pledge of Allegiance, and when we were done, our homeroom teacher shook her head.

"Now that was one of his worst jokes yet!" Ms. Ebear said, and we laughed. "I've got no other announcements, so please talk quietly among yourselves until the bell rings."

Avery, who sat in the seat next to me, turned to me.

"*Comment allez-vous?*" she asked.

"I have no idea what you just said," I replied.

"It means 'How are you?' in French," she replied. "I've been studying like crazy for that makeup quiz."

"*Muy bien,*" I said in Spanish, since that's the only other language I know.

"What did you do last night?" Avery asked.

"Well, after dinner I walked Zobe," I answered. "And then I did some more research on therapy dog training. I'm trying to convince Mom that Zobe should go. I think he'd be great."

Avery nodded. "I haven't met him yet. When are you going to invite me over?"

My schedule raced through mind. "Um, maybe Saturday? I'll let you know."

"That would be awesome," Avery said. "Show me a picture again."

We weren't allowed to use cell phones in class, but I had a picture of Zobe as my laptop wallpaper and I opened it up to show Avery. Soon a bunch of kids were surrounding me, trying to get a look at Zobe.

"What's all the fuss about?" Ms. Ebear asked, walking toward us, and I turned my laptop around to show her. She smiled. "A Great Dane? They are very sweet dogs."

"I know," I said. "I'm thinking of training him to become a therapy dog."

She nodded. "Sounds like a good idea," she replied, and then the bell rang.

I smiled, because now I had more ammunition for my mom. *Ms. Ebear thinks it's a good idea,* I could tell her. *And she's a teacher!*

But I didn't have much time to think about Zobe, because in each class, the teachers were overloading us with work. My first class was World History with Ms. Ebear, and we'd been studying African civilizations.

"I just posted the rubric for your Africa projects on the website," she announced at the beginning of class. "Along with the rubric, I've posted a schedule, because you are going to deliver this project to me in parts. So please review the schedule carefully."

Ms. Ebear was my favorite teacher, and that's one reason I was looking forward to doing the report. We each had to pick an African kingdom and research its art, religion, economy, and stuff like that. I am fascinated with how people lived in the past, but maybe that's because Ms. Ebear makes everything interesting.

Next I had Ms. Rashad's science class, where we had just started the life science curriculum, where we learn about the biology of plants, animals, and other organisms. She announced that we were going to have a big test on cells soon. In my fifth-period English class, Ms. Hamlin assigned us a novel to read, and said we were going to have to read a chapter a night *and* journal about it. And Señor Galarza, my Spanish teacher, gave us a pop quiz. It was an avalanche of schoolwork!

The only class where I felt less pressured was in fourth period gym, with Mr. Patel. The week before, we had been practicing formal dancing for an event at the school, and I'd hated every minute of it. But since Monday, we'd been playing volleyball.

I had never paid much attention to volleyball before. Since third grade, I'd been basketball-obsessed—partly because of my height, partly because I loved watching the WNBA, and partly because my brother, Jim, showed me how to play in our driveway just about as soon as I could walk.

In gym class, I'd quickly discovered that my

height was also an advantage in volleyball. Today, Mr. Patel had randomly divided us into teams of six. I got lucky, because I ended up on a team with a kid named Jacob, and four of my favorite people: Blake, Avery, Amanda, and Dylan, who'd been my partner for the dance and had been really sweet about it, considering I'm a foot taller than he is.

"Let Elle serve first!" Blake said, and nobody argued as we took our places on the court. I eyed the other team, which had Bianca, Natalie, and four guys from our class. It was going to be a competitive match.

Whomp! I sent the ball over the net with an over-hand serve and it whizzed past Bianca, landed in bounds, and bounced out.

"Whoo!" Blake cheered, and I served again. This time, one of the guys bumped it back and Amanda got to it, but she sent it careening out of bounds.

She looked at me and frowned. "Sorry," she said. "This just isn't my game. Basketball's the only thing I'm kind of good at, and I'm not great at that, either."

"You're getting much better at basketball!" I told her. "Don't sweat it. It's impossible to be good at everything. You should see me try to hit a softball."

Amanda smiled at me, and then Bianca served the ball to us. Dylan sent it floating over the top of the net, and Natalie spiked it right back to them, but Blake made an amazing play and dug it up with both hands. Avery hit it over the net, and it landed between two of the players.

I high-fived Blake and Avery. "Nice teamwork!"

We went on to win three of three games in gym, and that felt pretty great. I would say it was the highlight of my day, except the day wasn't over yet.

When the final bell rang, I headed over to the elementary school building, where Camp Cooperation was held, and quickly joined the other members of the team who were headed there (everyone but Avery, Tiff, and Caroline). We entered through the doors of the multipurpose room.

A guy in his twenties walked up to us, wearing jeans and a T-shirt with superheroes on it. "You must be the seventh grade basketball team!" he said. "I'm Brian, and that's Janette and Vicky." He pointed to two young women corralling a group of kids around a table.

We all introduced ourselves.

"Thanks for coming," Brian said. "We've got ten kids in the program, and it's always great to have extra help. We do activities for the first half hour, and then we have a snack."

"What do you want us to do?" Bianca asked.

"Just hang out with the kids," Brian said. "Some like to do art, others play board games, and I usually take a few outside to play catch or run around."

Natalie raised her hand. "I'll do some art," she said.

Brian smiled and nodded toward a little girl sitting at the table, wearing a pink shirt and matching headband. "Why don't you go say hi to Alyssa over there? She's going to love your hair."

Natalie had dyed her hair pink over the summer, so she and Alyssa were a perfect match. It took a few minutes to figure out what everybody else was going to do. I, of course, offered to go outside with Brian and the kids who liked sports.

Dina, Bianca, and I headed outside with Brian, two of the girls, and two of the boys.

"They're all different," Brian explained to us as we walked the short distance to the elementary school field, "but they all love being outside."

After Brian introduced us to the kids, he gave us a quick briefing about the kids we were with. Lily and Max both had some form of autism. Max was quiet and shy, and Lily was loud and energetic. The two others, Addie and Pete, had Down syndrome. Brian said they both had a lot of energy too.

I quickly found out that he was right. Once we got outside, eight-year-old Pete grabbed a yellow ball and ran up to me.

"Elle, Elle, play catch with me!" he said.

I smiled at him. I couldn't help it. He was so cute, wearing a jersey with the logo of the Wilmington Blue Rocks—Delaware's minor league baseball team.

"Sure," I said, and we moved out onto the field.

Pete threw the ball at me and it soared over my head, but I jumped up and caught it.

"Wow!" he said. "You're good at catch. Do you play baseball?"

"Nope," I said, tossing the ball back to him. "I play basketball."

His eyes lit up. "Oh, yeah! I've seen you."

"You have?" I asked, and he nodded.

"I go to the games," he said.

"Cool," I said, and caught the ball he threw to me. "Do *you* play baseball?"

He nodded. "I'm a good thrower. Not a good hitter. I like throwing."

We tossed the ball back and forth, and talked about the Wilmington Blue Rocks. Every once in a while I would glance over at the others. Lily and Bianca were kicking a soccer ball around the field, and Addie and Dina were playing catch too. Max stood next to Brian, looking at his feet.

I was telling Pete about my favorite player on the Blue Rocks when he interrupted me.

"Max likes to play quiet ball. We gotta play quiet ball with him," Pete said.

"Quiet ball?" I asked, puzzled. Pete grabbed my hand and pulled me toward Max and Brian.

"Max, we can play quiet ball," Pete said. "Elle can play with us. She's nice."

Max looked up, interested.

"Max, do you want to play with Pete and Elle?" Brian asked him.

Max nodded silently. Then Pete ran back out onto the field, and Max and I followed him.

"How do you play quiet ball?" I asked.

"Max doesn't like throwing," Pete said. "So you just run up and give him the ball, like this."

Pete ran up to Max and handed him the yellow ball. Max smiled. Then Pete ran about ten yards away from Max and faced him.

"Okay, Max, your turn!" Pete called out.

Max ran up to Pete and handed him the ball. Then he ran back to where he had been standing. I was starting to get the hang of quiet ball.

Next, Pete ran the ball to me. I had a sense that Max might not like me running toward him.

"Can I give you the ball, Max?" I asked, to make sure.

Max nodded, and I jogged over to him and handed him the ball. He smiled and ran to Pete.

I was pretty impressed with Pete. He had figured out the perfect game to play with his friend. Quiet ball wasn't the most exciting game in the world, but the two boys were having a great time.

Before we knew it, it was time for snack.

Brian and Janette asked us to help everyone wash their hands. Then we all had some water and apple slices. Pete ate his really fast and then tugged on my sleeve.

"Elle! Elle! Let's go play some more!" he said.

"In just a minute, Pete," Brian said. "We've got to wait for everybody else."

Pete frowned. "But I'm done!"

"Just another minute, pal," Brian said.

But Pete ran for the door. I quickly intercepted him.

"Hey, Pete, tell me again about the best batter on the Blue Rocks," I said.

Pete stopped short and started talking to me about his favorite team again, and Brian gave me a grateful smile.

We played outside some more after our snack, and the next thirty minutes just flew! When it was time to go, Brian approached me.

"You were really great with Pete and Max, Elle," he said.

"Thanks," I said. "My older sister has special needs, so I guess that helps make me comfortable around all kinds of people."

"Well, she must be a really great influence on you," Brian said. "Listen, if you ever have time to volunteer again, we'd love to have you come help out."

My mind started to whir. Volunteering here would be so much fun! Maybe I could do it on Tuesdays and Thursdays, when I didn't have practice.

Then I remembered about wanting to take Zobe to obedience class. I wasn't even sure how many days a week that class was, or when it met. Mom hadn't said yes to obedience class yet anyway, but I thought she might say yes to this. She'd have to, right? I mean, she's a regular champion for kids with special needs!

"I'd like that," I replied. "I'll let you know."

Then we headed over to the high school entrance, the school's official location for picking up kids from after-school activities. I found Avery waiting by the door.

"Sorry I never made it," she said. "How'd it go?"

"Awesome," I replied. "I played catch with this totally adorable boy named Pete. I think I want to go back and volunteer again, if my mom will let me."

Natalie chimed in from behind us. "It was *totally* fun," she said. "You were right, Elle, there was nothing to be nervous about."

"Cool," I said. "Maybe you can volunteer again with me sometime."

Natalie frowned. "I'd love to, but I don't know. There's so much homework this semester, don't you think?"

Before I could answer, Mom's car pulled up. I ran outside to meet her. I was tempted to ask her about the volunteering right away, but I decided to wait until dinner.

Sometimes, it helped to have Dad in my corner. He was a little less strict than Mom, and he might be able to help me convince her that I could handle this.

Sooooo Tired!

I didn't even have to bring up the subject of the after-school program at dinner. Mom did it for me.

"So, Elle, tell us, how did your service day go?" she asked.

"It was really great," I replied, cutting into my pork chop. "The kids there are all between the ages of six and eleven, and they're really fun and sweet. Most of them have autism, and a few have Down syndrome."

"Well, I'm really glad Coach Ramirez chose that program for your service day," Mom said. "I'm sure the kids were glad to have some energetic young women to play with."

"They were," I said. "In fact, one of the program leaders, Brian, said that I was so great with the kids that I could come volunteer any time I want to."

Dad beamed at me. "That's my Elle!" he said.

"So, I was thinking," I continued, "that maybe I could help out on Tuesdays and Thursdays, when I don't have practice."

Mom frowned, and to my surprise, Dad did too.

"Elle, that sounds like a big commitment," he said. "When will you have time to do your homework?"

"It'll be easy," I said. "The program is after school, so I can do homework after dinner."

"Maybe," Mom said. "But that's still a lot on your plate. When would you have any down time? I just don't know, honey."

"Come on," I said, nodding to Jim's empty chair. "Jim has football practice every single day now, and he doesn't get home until dark. And you don't think *he's* too busy."

"Jim is older than you," Mom said. "He's learned how to manage his time."

"I can learn!" I insisted.

"We'll think about it, Elle," Dad said.

I sighed and stood up. "Okay, I'm done. I'm going to start my homework."

I started to run upstairs, but Dad's voice stopped me.

"Aren't you forgetting something?" he asked.

I turned back to see Zobe at my heels, staring at me.

"Oh right!" I said. "Zobe's walk. No problem!"

"I don't know if I like you walking him this late," Mom said. "It's dark already."

"I'll text Blake," I said, and a few minutes later he and I were walking down the street toward the park, with Zobe on the leash. The park was closed after dark, but it was still nice to walk alongside it.

We were near the park entrance when Blake suddenly stopped and made a face.

"Um, Elle," he said, and he nodded behind me.

"Zobe just left a Great Dane–size present on the sidewalk."

"He what?" I asked, and I turned around to see Zobe smiling at me, right in front of a pile of poop. "Ugh! I forgot the poopy bags!"

"Poopy bags? Is that what they're called?" Blake asked. "That is hilarious."

"There is nothing funny about this," I said.

And then I saw Amanda walking toward us with her dog, Freckles, who was less than half the size of Zobe, with white and brown fur, droopy brown ears, and brown spots all across her white snout.

"Oh my gosh, Elle, is this Zobe?" Amanda asked. "He is awesome!"

"Yes, and he just made an *awesome* poop on the sidewalk," I said. "Do you have an extra poopy bag?"

"Of course," Amanda replied. She had hers in a little plastic holder attached to the leash, and she pulled one out for me. "Here you go."

Cleaning up after Zobe was one of my least favorite things about him, but I knew I had to do it to be a responsible dog owner. When I was finished, and the bag was in the trash, Amanda pulled some hand sanitizer from the pocket of her hoodie and handed it to me.

"Wow, you think of everything," I said.

Amanda shrugged. "We've had a dog in the family ever since I was a baby," she said.

I glanced over at Blake, who was busy doing something on his phone.

"So, do you always walk Freckles this late?" I asked.

"Not usually, but Freckles was whining to go out," she replied. "I think it was that taco she stole off my plate at dinner."

I laughed. "Zobe hasn't stolen any food yet. I'm surprised, actually. But he's pretty chill most of the time."

"He seems pretty chill," Amanda said, watching as Zobe and Freckles sniffed each other. "Anyway, I just live across the street."

She nodded toward a yellow house.

"Oh wow, I never realized you lived so close," I said.

"We should get the dogs together sometime," Amanda suggested, "for a doggy date."

"That's a great idea!" I said, and I could feel my cheeks flush a little, although I wasn't sure why.

Blake looked up from his phone. "Oh, hi, Amanda."

"She's been here for, like, five minutes," I said. "Who've you been texting?"

"Bianca," he replied.

My eyebrows shot up. "Bianca?"

When Blake and Bianca had been paired up for the dance, they ended up being really great partners. I suspected that maybe Bianca had a crush on Blake, or he had one on her. I couldn't blame him. I mean, she was a great athlete and really pretty, with her glossy black hair. And when she wasn't giving me attitude on the basketball team, she could be nice.

Blake shrugged. "Well, you know, she was my partner at the dance, and so we talk and stuff," he replied. "She had some questions about Ebear's history project."

"Oh, right!" I said. "I need to get home and do

my homework. I think Zobe's done what he came to do, anyway."

"I hope so," Blake said.

Amanda grinned. "See you tomorrow!"

We took off in different directions. I said good night to Blake, and after Zobe had a long drink from his water bowl we headed upstairs to start my homework. I pulled out all of my books, piled them on my desk, and opened my laptop.

I was supposed to study for science, read a chapter of the novel that Ms. Hamlin had assigned plus write a journal entry on it, and do a worksheet for Spanish. The outline of my history project for Ms. Ebear wasn't due until Monday.

I did the worksheet first; that was easy. Then I looked at my science notes for half an hour. I read the assigned chapter and started to yawn. I hadn't even showered yet! I looked at the schedule and saw that even though I was supposed to write a journal entry a day, they weren't all due for two weeks.

I can always write the journal entry tomorrow, I reasoned with myself. *And start my history project then too.*

Then I had the idea that I could make a spread-sheet and plan out when everything was due, so I wouldn't miss any deadlines. It was a good idea, but as soon as I opened the program on my computer, all of the rows and columns began to look blurry, and I yawned again. I shut the laptop and headed for the shower.

There's plenty of time, I assured myself. I had always gotten all my work done in sixth grade, and I'd played basketball then, too. I knew I could catch up. There was time this weekend.

After my shower, I said good night to Mom and Dad, and then I crashed, hard. It didn't even matter that Zobe was stretched out so big that there was almost no space for me on the bed. I curled up into a ball and fell asleep before I even had a chance to worry about the game coming up on Sunday, or wonder what Mom and Dad were going to decide about the volunteering.

Friday Night Lights

There you go, Elle! Staying focused! Great job!"

The rare words of praise from Coach Ramirez reached my ears as I jumped for the basket, but I didn't let them distract me. The ball bounced off the backboard and sank into the net with a satisfying swish.

Avery slapped my hand as we made our way back down the court. It was Friday, practice day, and after a bunch more footwork drills we were having another scrimmage.

Me, Avery, Patrice, Hannah, and Natalie were facing Bianca, Tiff, Amanda, Dina, and Caroline. Dina had control of the ball now and was making her way toward the basket, dodging and weaving between us defenders. Then she threw it to Bianca, but I jumped up and intercepted. I took it down the court and made a layup—without traveling or tripping over my feet.

Coach blew her whistle. "Great job, everybody! See you all at the big game tonight!"

I ran into the locker room to get my backpack, because I knew Mom would already be waiting for me. The "big game" was the varsity football game, the last home game at Spring Meadow, and also senior night. Since my brother was a senior, that meant Mom and Dad would get to walk down the field with him at the start of the game, so it was important.

But as I was sprinting away, I felt Coach's hand on my shoulder.

"Elle, can I talk to you for a sec?" she asked.

I stopped. "Sure," I replied. Everyone else disappeared into the locker room.

"I saw some improvement today, Elle," Coach said. "Keep working hard. You have the potential to be one of the best offensive players I've ever seen at this age level. If you continue to focus, you could carry this team to the championships."

"Thanks," I said, and I was feeling a little bit stunned. Me? Carry the team to the championships? That was a lot of pressure. "I'll . . . I'll keep working hard, I promise."

"I'm counting on you, Elle," Coach said, and then she let me dash off to get my backpack. I waved good-bye to my friends and hurried outside to the pickup spot, where Mom was waiting for me.

"Mom!" I cried as I slid into the front seat. Her blond hair was shiny and sleek, not pulled back in a bun or a ponytail, like usual. And she had eye shadow and mascara decorating her bright blue eyes.

"I know!" she said. "Gary at the salon went a little too far. But it's a special night, and there are going to be lots of pictures taken, so I thought I needed some professional help. Do I look ridiculous?"

"No, you look beautiful!" I said. "You just don't look like *you*, you know what I mean?"

Mom nodded. "I know," she said.

"Is Beth coming?" I asked. It was difficult for Beth to be around crowds, especially at outdoor events, because the smells and the temperature really bothered her. But we tried to bring her to important events whenever it worked out.

"Dad and I talked about it, but since we'll both be busy on the field for a while, she's going to stay home with Kim," Mom said, naming one of Beth's babysitters.

I frowned. "That stinks. Couldn't I watch her?"

"Maybe another time, but it's going to be hectic down at the field," Mom said. "Don't worry, Jim's got a lot more events this year. Senior awards, prom, graduation . . ."

I understood, but it was one of the sad things about Beth's needs. Sometimes it meant she couldn't do all of the same things we did, and that just didn't seem fair.

We pulled into our driveway.

"Take a fast shower, Elle!" Mom called up to me. "We've got to get down to the field early. And wear something nice!"

I came back downstairs fifteen minutes later with my wet hair pulled back into a ponytail. I had on a pair of dark jeans and my newest hooded sweatshirt with no holes or stains or anything.

Dad was in the living room, wearing dress pants and a green sweater over a pale yellow button-down shirt (Nighthawks colors).

"You ready, Elle?" he asked.

Before I could answer, Zobe jumped up on me.

"Just gotta feed Zobe," I replied, and ran into the kitchen, past Mom, who was coming out.

"Elle! Is that what you're wearing?" she asked.

"It's my nicest sweatshirt!" I protested as I filled Zobe's bowl with kibble. "Besides, I'm not walking out onto the field with Jim. Just you guys."

Mom sighed. "I don't have time to argue. We'll meet you out in the car."

I said good-bye to Zobe and Beth and we headed out. Because Spring Meadow is a small private school, we share a football field with a college in Wilmington. When we got there, people were just starting to arrive for the seven p.m. game. The Nighthawks marching band was warming up in the parking lot, and as we walked down the path to the field, I could see green and yellow balloons tied to the railings of the bleachers.

Then, as we walked farther down the path, I saw stakes stuck in the ground. Each one had the name, number, and photo of a senior on it.

"Look, there's Jim!" I said, running to his sign. "I need a selfie!"

I crouched down, whipped out my phone, and took a photo of me with Jim's sign. I was starting to get excited, and a little sad. I couldn't believe this was Jim's last game before the playoffs. And after this year was over, he'd be going off to college! I saw Mom getting teary-eyed as she looked at the sign, and I knew she was thinking the same thing.

We kept walking and passed the concession stand, which we all call the Snack Shack. A bunch of kids were already on line, buying drinks and chips.

Mom's friend, Mrs. Friedman, waved us over.

"Jeni! Eddie! You two look fantastic!" she said. "I wish I could get out of here to see you walk the field, but we're short-handed tonight. You'll have to show me the pictures."

"Of course, Gina," Mom replied.

Then Mrs. Friedman turned to me. "Elle! You're old enough to help now. Maybe you could come back and help us during halftime? I don't want you to miss any of your brother's game."

"Uh, sure," I said. I had never helped out at the Snack Shack before, but it looked easy enough.

Then a bunch of the other senior parents swarmed around Mom and Dad, and I headed off to the bleachers. I found Avery sitting with Hannah and Natalie. Like me, everyone was wearing a Nighthawks hoodie. Natalie's cheeks were painted with green and yellow stripes.

"Nice paint job!" I told her.

Natalie grinned. "Thanks. I've always wanted to do this, and I had some makeup crayons leftover from Halloween."

Then the PA system crackled. "Before our game begins tonight, Spring Meadow School is going to honor its senior football players and cheerleaders," Principal Lubin announced. "Let's give them all a big hand!"

We all stood up and started cheering. One by one, the seniors and their parents walked through a big balloon arch on the field, stopped at the fifty-yard line, and posed for a picture. I saved my loudest cheering for Jim and my parents, and of course, my friends helped me.

"Go, Jim!"

"Yay, Delucas!"

Then the balloon arch was whisked away, and we stood while the marching band played the national anthem, and the game against the Pottsville Pirates began. I kept my eyes on Jim the whole first half. His coach had him playing tight end on the offensive line—because Jim is big but he's also fast and good at catching passes. Every time Jim caught the ball and moved it down the field, I went crazy.

When the clock ran down at halftime, the score

was Nighthawks 13, Pirates 7. I cheered for Jim as he ran off the field—and then I remembered my promise to help out with the Snack Shack.

"Mrs. Friedman asked me to help at the shack," I told my friends. "I'll be back after halftime."

"Bring me back some popcorn!" Avery called out.

I pushed my way through the crowd and entered the Snack Shack through the back. Mrs. Friedman nodded when she saw me.

"Elle, you're on drinks," she said. "Just give each customer the drinks they need and send them on down the line to pay."

"Okay," I said, and moved in front of two giant plastic garbage cans filled with ice and water, soda, and sports drinks. I didn't have time to process any of this when the next person on line, a boy about nine years old, came up to the counter.

"Blue sports drink," he said.

I dug through the garbage can and pulled a blue sports drink out of the ice.

"Not dark blue," he said, "light blue."

"What's the difference?" I asked.

"Light blue tastes better," he said.

I dug back into the can and found a light blue drink and handed it to him. It looked only slightly different from the dark blue.

Up next was a dad who needed three waters, one soda, and one blue sports drink.

"Dark blue or light blue?" I asked.

"What's the difference?" he said.

I shrugged. "I honestly don't know." I reached in and grabbed the first blue drink I saw and handed it to him.

The line never seemed to end. My hands started to get numb from plunging them into the ice over and over again. Finally, Mrs. Friedman came by and tapped me on the shoulder.

"Thanks for helping, Elle," she said. "Now go back and watch your brother's game."

I hurried back to the bleachers.

"Where's my popcorn?" Avery asked.

I groaned. "Oh man, I'm sorry! It's insane in there. I never knew what Mom went through when she worked the shack."

Hannah nudged me. "Is that your brother with the ball?"

I looked down on the field. There was Jim, running down the field with two Pirates on his heels. I leaped to my feet.

"Go, Jim!" I yelled. "Go, go, go!"

Jim rocketed down the field for a total of forty-three yards, all the way into the end zone.

"TOUCHDOWN!" I screamed at the top of my lungs, and Avery hugged me. We started jumping up and down.

By the end of the game, which the Nighthawks won 28–14, my voice was hoarse from screaming for Jim. I ran down to the field so I could slap his hand as he made his way back to the locker room. I held my hand out, and he stepped out of line and gave me a big squeeze. A big, sweaty squeeze. Then he put me down and jogged off with the rest of the team.

That's when I actually started to cry. What was I going to do when my big brother went off to college? I was going to miss him so much!

I felt Dad's hand on my shoulder. "Come on, Elle, it's late. Jim will meet us back home."

Mom, Dad, and I were all quiet on the ride home. I knew they must be feeling happy and sad at the same time, like I was. But it wasn't an easy thing for any of us to talk about.

When we got home and Mom opened the front door, Zobe bounded out and jumped up on me.

"I should walk him," I said, yawning.

"Just bring him out in the backyard, Elle," Dad said. "I think that's the best thing to do from now on, since it's getting dark so early."

I didn't argue. I went outside with Zobe and played a quick game of catch with him before going back inside. I was sweaty from all the cheering, excitement, and working in the Snack Shack, so I took another shower.

I wanted to stay awake until Jim came home from celebrating with the team, but I couldn't. I was exhausted. I fell asleep, dreaming of my brother running over the goal line with the football in his hand.

A Surprise in the Stands

I woke up the next morning to the sound of my cell phone pinging. I'd been so tired the night before that I'd forgotten to shut it off and charge it.

I picked it up and saw that it was 10:17 a.m., I had thirteen percent battery left, and Avery had texted me.

Can I come meet Zobe today?

I stared at the text for a minute, blinking. Zobe! I needed to feed him and take him for his morning walk.

My mind raced as I tried to figure out how to

answer Avery's question. After I walked Zobe, I still had homework to do. I hadn't gotten any done yesterday because of Jim's game.

I really wanted to hang with Avery, but I knew I had to focus on school. If Avery came over, we would end up talking or binge watching that dating show that she likes, and I wouldn't get anything done.

Sorry, I texted back. **Can't today, busy with homework. Maybe next week?**

👍 Avery replied. Then she sent me a gif of a dog jumping up to catch a ball in his mouth.

My stomach rumbled, and I realized how hungry I was. I threw on sweatpants and a T-shirt and went downstairs, where the smell of bacon made my stomach rumble again. I found Jim in the kitchen, cooking a mountain of bacon in one frying pan and another mountain of eggs in the other.

"Mom and Dad are in Philly with Beth, seeing one of her specialists," Jim told me. "Dad told me to tell you he walked Zobe this morning. But he wants you to walk him again at lunchtime. After you fold the laundry."

I nodded. "Sure. I just need to eat something."

"Too bad I didn't make extra," Jim said, and then he grinned. "Come on, eat with me."

"Great game last night," I told him as we both sat down at the kitchen table, our plates full of food.

"Thanks!" he said. "There was terrific energy on the field, you know?"

I nodded. "I felt it."

"I'm going to try to go to your game tomorrow," Jim said. "I haven't seen you play yet this season."

I laughed. "You're not missing much. Except me always messing up because I can't control my own legs."

"You know that the same thing happened to me too, Elle," Jim said. "This won't last forever. Don't sweat it."

I was grateful to Jim for saying that, but I felt a twinge of sadness at the same time. A year from now, he wouldn't be around to make me breakfast and give me pep talks.

I finished my eggs and bacon and stood up. "I'm

going to go fold that laundry," I said. "Need help cleaning up?"

"Nah, I got it," Jim replied.

I went to the laundry room and picked up a big basket of clean laundry—sheets and towels that I brought upstairs to my room to fold because it's easiest to do when I can spread it out on my bed. I played some music on my phone as it was charging, and I got into a decent groove. Then I put everything away in the linen closet.

By the time I was done, Zobe was restlessly following me, so I took him for a quick walk to the park. I still needed to get my homework going, so I didn't ask Blake to come with me.

Believe it or not, I was hungry again when I got back, so I made a sandwich. My parents still weren't home, but I knew that Beth's doctor appointments could take a long time, and the traffic from our town in Delaware to Philly could be brutal.

After my sandwich, Zobe and I settled down in my room. The first thing I did was try to schedule out my homework. I had to read two extra chapters of the novel over the weekend to catch up, and my history project outline was due Monday. I decided to read first to get that out of the way.

I had finished one chapter when Jim knocked on my door, a basketball clutched under his arm.

"Hey, do you want to do some drills with me?" he asked. "I mean, if you've got time."

I didn't have time, really. But I'd been so bummed out, thinking about Jim going off to college, that I couldn't say no.

I slammed my book shut. "Just for a little while," I said. "I'm supposed to be doing homework."

Zobe jumped up too—he wanted to come with us, but I had to disappoint him.

"Sorry, Zobe," I told him. "The hoop is out front, and I can't have you running around outside without a leash."

I swear he frowned at me, like he knew exactly what I had just said.

Outside, Jim showed me some drills he remembered from his basketball days. They were pretty much like the ones Coach Ramirez had shown us, but it was more fun doing them with Jim.

We hadn't been drilling for long when Blake appeared, holding a basketball under his arm.

"Jim's showing me some drills," I said. "Want to join us?"

"I thought you'd never ask," Blake said. "I am totally bored today."

"I'll guard the basket, and you two take turns trying to make layups," Jim suggested.

I dribbled toward the basket first. Normally, I can't get past Jim. But now that I was six feet tall, it was easier. I jumped up as high as I could and sent the ball swishing through the net.

Blake and I took turns trying to get past Jim, trash-talking each other and laughing the whole time. Then a horn honked. Mom and Dad were pulling into the driveway in the minivan.

Sweaty and panting, Jim, Blake, and I stood aside. When Dad stopped the car we helped get Beth and her wheelchair out of the van.

"How'd it go?" Jim asked.

"Just a long day of testing," Mom said. "Beth was missing Zobe, though. She kept signing 'dog' to me."

"Aw!" I said. I leaned down to greet Beth. Then I nodded to Blake. "See you later."

"Back to boredom!" he said, and dribbled his basketball back home.

I wheeled Beth inside. "Zobe awaits!"

I spent some quality time with Zobe and Beth while Dad made dinner—his specialty, Italian food, which he always cooks for me the night before a game. It's our tradition. Pretty soon the house smelled like garlic, basil, and tomatoes, and my stomach was growling again. Luckily, Dad called out that it was dinner time before the growls got loud enough to scare Zobe.

Dad had made chicken parmesan, spaghetti marinara, garlic bread, and a salad. I don't like to eat much on a game morning—just half a bagel with peanut butter, to give me energy without weighing me down. But the night before a game I eat a big meal, to make sure I've got enough energy in reserve. I don't know if it's scientific, but it seems to work for me.

That night's dinner was delicious, and we all talked about Jim's exciting touchdown. When it was done, I ran around with Zobe in the backyard, showered, and put on pjs. I climbed into bed and picked up my book for English again, but my eyes started to droop.

Game tomorrow morning, I reminded myself. *Better get some sleep.*

Then I put down my book, set my alarm for 6:30, and conked out.

Beep! Beep! Beep! Beep!

I groaned at the sound of the alarm, and then I felt a warm tongue on my cheek.

"Come on, Zobe," I said. "You're part of the pregame routine now."

I'd been doing my own ritual before the game, ever since I'd read that WNBA players all have them. Normally, I'd wake up at seven, but now I had to work Zobe into the mix.

I threw on some sweats and headed outside with Zobe on his leash for a quick walk to the park. Then I fed Zobe and headed outside for thirty minutes of informal shootaround practice in the driveway. After that I showered, ate my half a bagel with peanut butter, and then napped for half an hour. The rest of my family knows this whole routine by heart, so nobody bothered me while I was doing it.

By 10:15 I was awake again, and got dressed for the game. I put on my jersey. Then I put on my socks and shoes. *Then* I put my right foot through one leg of my shorts, and then my left foot through the other. That's because I wanted to make sure I started off each game on the right foot.

At 10:30, Mom, Dad, Jim, and I piled into the van to drive to the game. Our first game had been away, but this time the Edgewood Eagles were coming to our gym at Spring Meadow. My right knee bounced up and down with nervous energy as we got closer to the school. I had to prove to everyone that I was not Runaway Train!

When we entered the gym, Mom gave me a hug. "You'll do great!" she said.

Jim fist-bumped me. "Don't worry, Elle. You're gonna kill it out there."

Dad grinned. "I agree!"

"Thanks!" I said, and then I ran out onto the court, where the team was warming up. I grabbed a ball and started dribbling when I heard a familiar voice from the stands.

"Elle! Elle! I see you!"

I looked up to see Pete, the kid from the after-school program. I remembered him telling me that he came to the games.

"Hi, Pete!" I called back.

Caroline walked up to me. "My brother loves you," she said.

"Your brother?" I asked. Then it hit me. "Pete is your brother?"

She grinned. "Yeah," she replied. "He had fun with you at Camp Cooperation. He was so excited today when we were getting ready for the game. He kept saying, 'I get to see Elle!'"

"Aw, that's sweet," I said. "I had fun hanging out with him."

"He's a super sports freak," she said. "He's the one who kept saying I should join the team last year."

Then she frowned. "Too bad I'm always on the bench."

I wanted to say something to make Caroline feel better, because Coach did keep her on the bench most of the time, and I wasn't sure if that was fair. But before I could say anything, Coach Ramirez called out to us.

"Two lines, girls! Shooting drill!"

We quickly split up into two groups of five and lined up on the free throw lane lines. The first two players ran up to the free throw line and took turns shooting. Then each player ran to the back of the other line—the line they hadn't started from. This way, everyone got to take shots from both sides of the baskets. We kept doing that, running and shooting, until the ref blew his whistle, signaling the start of the game.

Coach Ramirez called us together. "Okay, I want Elle on center; Bianca's my shooting guard; Avery, point guard; Tiff, power forward; and Patrice, you're my small forward. Let's do this!"

We all clapped hands and yelled out, "Nighthawks!" Then the five of us jogged out onto the court.

I lined up across from the Eagles center for the tip-off at center court. As usual, I stood almost a foot taller than the other center. The ref approached us.

"Ready?" he asked, and we both nodded.

He tossed the ball up, and I jumped up and grabbed it with both hands. I saw Avery streak past me like lightning, so I passed it to her. She dribbled it a few feet, then stopped as one of the Eagles came toward her. She passed it sideways to Bianca, who dribbled it to the basket for a layup. Two points Nighthawks!

That first move got my blood pumping, and I was excited about the way we were playing like a team. The Eagles had the ball next, and I jumped up and stopped a girl from making a shot. I passed the ball to Tiff, who dribbled it up to the three-point arc and made a perfect shot. Nighthawks 5, Eagles 0!

Our great start took a slight detour when we had control of the ball next and Bianca made a shot that bounced off the rim. I think all ten players went for the rebound, but my height gave me an advantage and I scooped it out of the air. Three Eagles immediately surrounded me and raised their arms in the air to block me, so I quickly crouched down and passed it between them, right to Patrice, who was clear.

Patrice grabbed it with both hands and dribbled it away from the basket to get clear. Then she stopped and began to set up her shot, but changed her mind when her defender got too close, so she started dribbling again. The ref blew his whistle. Patrice had put two hands on the ball, so she wasn't supposed to dribble again. The Eagles got the ball.

It was kind of a rookie mistake, even though I know we're only in seventh grade. I wondered if maybe she was feeling extra pressure because her mom was our coach; I know that would stress me out. In any case, the Eagles scored after that, and we ended the quarter 5–2.

Coach Ramirez kept me in after that, and even though she switched out Hannah for Bianca and Caroline for Tiff, she kept in Patrice. That made no sense to me at all, because Patrice wasn't really playing her best.

Even so, I was happy to see Caroline off the bench. The first time I got the ball Caroline was open, so I passed it to her. She dribbled it up to the basket and made a shot, but it bounced off the rim. Hannah got it back and quickly sank it.

I scored three times in the second quarter—once when we had control of the ball, and once when one of the Eagles elbowed me and I got to shoot a free throw.

When halftime came, I was panting and sweaty, and the score was Nighthawks 14, Eagles 8. Coach kept me out for the third quarter, because league rules specify that no player can play more than three quarters in a game, unless the team is short players. Both teams scored in the third quarter, but we still kept a strong lead: 21–14.

Coach Ramirez put me back in the game in the fourth quarter. I bolted onto the court, excited to finish the game. In the first five minutes, I got a traveling violation. This time, I pivoted on my right foot to turn away from an Eagles defender. But then I lifted up my right foot when I turned around again to face the basket.

"Focus, Elle!" Coach yelled.

I grimaced, and I let it get to me. A few minutes later, Avery passed me the ball from the sidelines. I spun around to avoid the Eagles player covering me and lost my balance. I fell forward on my knees, and the ball spilled out of my hands and one of the Eagles picked it up. I felt awful. But Coach kept me in until the end, even though our lead narrowed. And we still won the game, 30–26.

After the game, Pete ran down the bleachers to hug Caroline. Then he gave me a big hug too!

"Great job, Elle!" he said.

"Thanks, Pete," I replied, and then I noticed Mom and Dad had come down from the bleachers and were behind us.

"Are you coming back to see us?" Pete asked.

"I don't know," I said. "I'm waiting to find out if I can."

I looked at my parents. "This is Pete, from the

after-school program. He's Caroline's brother."

"Nice to meet you, Pete," Dad said, and shook his hand. Then Pete ran back to his parents.

Mom and Dad exchanged glances.

"I suppose you can give volunteering a try, Elle," Mom said. "It sounds like a wonderful program."

"As long as you keep up with your schoolwork," Dad said.

I smiled. "I will! I promise!"

Avery ran up to us. "Everyone's going for pizza. Mom said she'll drive us."

I looked at my parents again.

"Go!" Mom said. "Have fun!"

I gave her a sweaty hug and left the gym with Avery. Soon we were in Sal's Pizzeria, diving into the pies that Coach Ramirez had ordered ahead for us. Since I had only had my usual half-bagel breakfast that morning, I wolfed mine down.

I had taken a seat next to Caroline, because I wanted to tell her the good news that I was allowed to volunteer for Camp Cooperation.

"So Mom and Dad said I could do it," I told her.

"Do you volunteer every Tuesday and Thursday?"

"When I can," she replied. Then she paused. "Don't you have a special needs sister?"

"Beth," I replied. "She's my big sister. She's got CP and autism, and she's deaf and blind."

Caroline nodded thoughtfully. "I think I've seen her with you guys at some of the school events."

"Yeah, she goes to the big ones," I said.

"I guess we're lucky that Pete can do just about everything with us," she said. "Does Beth ever have to go to the hospital? Because Pete had heart surgery when he was a baby. . . ."

I felt Avery tap me on the shoulder. "Elle, I found that video I was telling you about the other day," she said. "The one with the baby that dumps spaghetti on his head and then acts so innocent. It's so cute!"

"What?" I gave Caroline a look of apology and watched the video on Avery's phone. It was totally adorable—but I felt bad for not finishing the conversation with Caroline. I wanted to tell her about the surgeries that Beth had had, and how scary that was, worrying that she was going to be all right.

By the time Avery's mom drove us home, it was almost 2:30. I walked Zobe, and then I spent some time with Beth outside since it was such a beautiful day. Then Mom made an awesome dinner of salmon nicoise salad, loaded with potatoes and green beans and lettuce. It was just what I needed after my greasy pizza lunch.

I was helping clear the table when it hit me like a bolt of lightning—my history project! The outline was due tomorrow.

"Gotta do homework!" I said, jumping up. After I took Zobe to the backyard, I brought him up to my bedroom, closed the door, and got to work.

I had thought the outline would be easy, but I was wrong. I had to choose an African kingdom I was interested in, research it, and give specific details about key people, places, and achievements in an outline. The rubric said I needed three points of detail for each topic, but it was so late and I was so tired that I didn't get everything done that I needed to.

But it's just an outline, I told myself, yawning. *Ms. Ebear knows I'm going to do a good job on the project. This should be fine.* I closed my laptop.

And once again, I fell asleep earlier than usual and as soon as my head hit the pillow.

Falling

T oday in *fall* news, there is falling rain outside, and falling leaves," Principal Lubin announced over the PA system the next morning. "Enjoy the fall, but please don't fall asleep in class or fall behind on your work!"

The word "asleep" made me yawn—I couldn't help it. I felt like no matter how long I slept these days, it wasn't enough. In an eerie way, it felt like the principal's warning was just for me.

I didn't fall asleep in homeroom, although I did spend most of it staring out the window, watching the raindrops hit the red leaves of the maple tree outside. It was hypnotic, and I yawned again.

Next to me, Avery yawned. "Stop doing that, Elle!" she hissed. "Don't you know that yawns are contagious? When you see somebody yawn, it makes you yawn too."

"Really? Is that scientific?" I asked, and I yawned in the middle of the word. "Oh. Maybe you're right!"

The bell rang, and Avery left for her class while I stayed behind for World History with Ms. Ebear.

"All right, everybody! Time to hand in your outlines!" she said. "I can't wait to read all of your thoughtful and amazing ideas."

My stomach flipped a little. *Thoughtful and amazing?* I would not use those words to describe my outline. But there was nothing I could do about it now, except do a better job on the other parts of the project.

It must have been the rain, because I dragged around all morning. I got my energy back during gym, when we played volleyball again. Mr. Patel told me that I had a "killer serve!" That felt pretty good.

But my stomach flipped again in English class.

"You should all have five entries in your journals by now," Ms. Hamlin told the class. "On Wednesday I'll be doing a journal check, so make sure you are up to date."

Five entries? I hadn't even done one! And since we were supposed to do a journal entry every weeknight, I'd have to do a total of seven journal entries before she checked us on Wednesday. I started to panic, but again, what could I do?

When school was over, I had basketball practice. The rain had ended, and my sneakers squished on the muddy field as I walked to the high school gym. When I walked to the locker room, I saw that Coach Ramirez had the TV set up again.

"Oh boy," I said out loud, and Amanda heard me.

"I know, right?" she said. "Watching my mistakes makes me cringe."

"Me too," I said. "Especially since last time Coach showed, like, a hundred things I did wrong."

"It wasn't a hundred!" Amanda said. "And anyway, you played great yesterday. I'm sure she won't have much to say about you at all."

She smiled at me, and I noticed the cute way she crinkled her freckled nose when she did. I smiled back.

"Thanks, I hope so," I said.

But fifteen minutes later, when we were all suited up and seated on the bleachers, I got a real surprise.

"You had a victory again on Sunday," Coach Ramirez began. "But *everyone* could have done better."

Coach fast-forwarded to the part where I caught the rebound, got mobbed, and then passed the ball to Patrice. I thought she was going to point out how Patrice had dribbled after holding the ball with two hands. But she didn't.

"Elle, you passed to Patrice, but Tiff was open on your left," she said, pointing to Tiff on the screen. "When you have possession of the ball, I need you to think quickly and weigh your passing options. Don't just pass to the closest player."

I couldn't believe what I was hearing. Yes, Tiff was open, but so was Patrice. What exactly was the problem?

She moved right past Patrice's penalty, and

stopped to compliment some of Bianca's footwork. Then, when we got to the second quarter, she
stopped when I passed the ball to Caroline.

"See? There you go again, Elle," she said. "You
should have passed it to Hannah here, not Caroline.
Hannah was in a better position to score."

I bit my lip and studied the screen. Coach had
a point. Hannah had no defenders around her and
was closer. But Caroline was open, and I admit that I
passed it to her because she hardly ever gets to play.
I guess I had been thinking with my heart instead of
my brain on that one.

I caught Amanda's eye, and she gave me a look
that showed she felt sorry for me. Which was nice,
but it didn't make me feel better. I looked away, and
zoned out as Coach continued through the tape.

I came out of my trance when I heard Coach
say my name again. "If Elle had kept her balance
here, we wouldn't have lost control of the ball." She
was pointing to the screen, to a frozen image of me
fallen on my knees.

My cheeks started to burn. Did she really have

to show that scene? How exactly was that going to make us play better as a team?

Thankfully, that was the last thing Coach pointed out, and we started warm-ups and drills. I focused on the physicality of what I was doing, enjoying the feel of my muscles and the sweat on my neck. I didn't want to think about that review tape.

After practice, I quickly grabbed my backpack and hurried out of the locker room. I didn't feel like talking to anybody, but Amanda ran up to me.

"Sorry I was wrong about Coach," she said.

I shrugged.

"Anyway, I was wondering if we should have a doggy date tomorrow, after school?" she asked.

"That would be nice," I said, and then I remembered. "But I can't! I'm volunteering for Camp Cooperation tomorrow."

Amanda frowned.

"Maybe Saturday?" I suggested.

"That could work," she replied, smiling again.

Then I heard Avery's voice behind me.

"Elle!" she called out, running up to us. "You rushed out of the locker room."

"Yeah, well, that wasn't exactly my favorite practice," I said.

She nodded sympathetically. "I know," she said. "But maybe Coach is being harder on you because you're such a good player."

I sighed. "Maybe. But it doesn't feel that way."

"So, can I come meet Zobe tomorrow?" Avery asked.

We were back outside now. The rain had turned the air chilly, and I zipped up my hoodie.

"I'm going back to Camp Cooperation to volunteer," I said.

"Aw, I'm never going to get to meet Zobe," she complained.

"You will, I promise," I said. "But volunteering is really important to me. The kids were so happy to have us there. It was such a good feeling."

"I understand," Avery said. "Then send me a

picture of Zobe today when you get home, okay?"

"Okay," I replied, and we fell into step together across the field.

Avery is such a good friend. The best. I knew I had to make time for her. But how was I supposed to do that when my life was so busy?

Somebody Who Understands

Elle's back! Elle's back! Hi, Elle!"

The next day, Pete ran up to me and hugged me as soon as I walked into the multipurpose room at the elementary school.

"Pete, am I invisible?" asked Caroline, who was standing right next to me.

Pete hugged her. "You're always back, Caroline."

"Well, I'm happy to see Elle back, too," Brian said. "I'm glad you could fit us into your schedule."

"Yeah, me too," I replied, although I wasn't

exactly sure if "fitting" was the right word. "Squeez-ing" was more like it.

"Pete would never forgive me if I didn't assign you to play outside," Brian said. "Caroline, is that okay with you?"

"That's fine," she said, and she pointed to a little red-haired girl sitting at the table. "I need to chal-lenge Meg at Candy Land. She beat me last time."

So I went back outside with Brian, Pete, Max, Lily, and Addie. The two girls kicked a soccer ball back and forth, and Pete and I played catch. Max wasn't in the mood to play quiet ball, but Brian said that was okay. Max just liked being outside.

The hour went really fast, and before I knew it, Caroline and I were outside, waiting for our rides to show up, while Pete ran in circles around us. My phone beeped.

"Mom says there's a traffic jam on Willow Street," I told Caroline. "She's going to be a few minutes late. I bet your mom is too."

She nodded. "At least it's nice out. Not chilly like yesterday."

My eyes traveled to Pete. "He is so cute," I said.

"Yeah," she replied. "You know, I have another brother, Sam, who's ten. They're both cute. And they both annoy me equally."

I thought about that. Jim annoyed me sometimes, like when he leaves his dirty football socks in the bathroom, or when he used to tease me for not brushing my hair. But Beth? I don't know if I could say that Beth annoyed me the way another sister might.

"I guess it's different for me," I said. "Beth has more challenges than Pete, you know, and also, she's my older sister. Mostly I worry that she's going to be okay. Like when you said Pete'd had surgery—Beth had a bunch when I was very little. It was scary."

"I know," Caroline said. "Pete's been okay since his heart surgery, but it still scares me to think I could lose him. I don't know what I'd do without him."

I felt tears forming in my eyes. I had never really been able to talk to anybody the way Caroline and I were talking right now. Avery and Blake were amazing listeners, and they loved Beth, but they didn't know what it felt like to have Beth as a sister. Jim did, but he and I never really talked about stuff like that. And Mom and Dad—they talked to me about Beth, but it wasn't the same.

"I think the same thing about Beth," I told Caroline. "I worry so much sometimes. And it bugs me when people say stuff like, 'Oh, it must be so hard for you, to have a sister who needs so much care.' Like Beth is a burden or something. She's not a burden. She's my sister and I love her."

"Now you're making me cry," Caroline said, and she wiped a tear away from her cheek—and then she laughed. "Although sometimes it's not easy taking care of Pete. Mom's always asking me to play with him, and help him with his homework. And then I have to help Sam, too."

"Oh right, you're the oldest," I realized. Mom and Dad never gave me any responsibilities for Beth. Maybe they thought they were doing me a favor, but what if they didn't trust me to have more responsibilities? Just like they didn't trust me to take Zobe to obedience class, or how they hadn't wanted me to volunteer after school.

They didn't seem to mind when I spent seven days a week training for or playing basketball. But I knew there was more to life than basketball, and I wanted to do that stuff, too. I didn't want to have to devote my life to one thing, just because I was good at it. And was I even good at it anymore? I wasn't so sure.

As these thoughts were running through my head, Mom's minivan pulled up and I waved good-bye to Caroline and Pete.

"See you tomorrow!"

"Bye, Elle!" Pete said. "Bye, bye, Elle!"

Pete's voice instantly cheered me up. "Bye, Pete!" I called out, and I climbed into the passenger seat.

Mom looked at me. "My goodness, Elle, I haven't seen you smile like that in a while," she said. "This volunteering is good for you."

"Yeah, it is," I replied, and I realized something: People always thought volunteering was supposed to make other people feel good. But it worked the opposite way, too. Volunteering with those kids had made me feel really happy. I hadn't even thought about the bummer practice of the day before.

I had time before dinner to work on my journal entries for English. I'd managed to finish four on Monday night, after practice, so now I had three more to go. I knew I was rushing them, but a journal was supposed to be about your feelings, right? And right now, my feelings were rushed.

I still hadn't finished my homework in time for dinner, but before I went up to my room, there was something I wanted to do.

"Come on, Zobe," I said. "Let's hang outside with Beth for a while."

First I signed the word "outside" to Beth in her hand, and she nodded her head. Then I wheeled her out, with Zobe right at my heels.

I picked up Zobe's red rubber ball and threw it across the lawn. He ran after it, and came back with it in his mouth. Then he dropped it into Beth's lap. I couldn't believe it!

Beth reached out and touched Zobe's head.

She nodded her head up and down, and I knew she understood that Zobe was playing with her.

I picked up the ball and threw it again, and Zobe fetched it and once more deposited it on Beth's lap. I laughed.

"Good boy, Zobe!" I said. Then, remembering Avery's request, I snapped a photo of Zobe and Beth and sent it to her.

Dad came out a few minutes later. "Would you look at that?" he said. He walked over to Zobe and started scratching him behind both ears. "What a good dog you are, Zobe!"

Then he looked at me. "You may be on to something, Elle, with the idea of Zobe becoming a therapy dog."

"It's a great idea, right?" I asked.

"I'll look into it," Dad promised. "I just worry that you're too busy with school and basketball."

School! I knew I had to get back in and do homework.

"Can you stay outside with Zobe and Beth for a little longer?" I asked Dad. "I have to finish my homework, and I don't think Beth's ready to stop playing with Zobe.

"Of course, Elle," Dad said.

I headed back inside, wishing I didn't have to leave. But I had to get more focused about doing my homework. I knew I had to do a better job than I'd done on my history project outline. I still hadn't gotten it back from Ms. Ebear.

Maybe it won't be so bad, I thought, and then I curled up on my bed with my English book and started to read.

Don't They Know I Have a Life?

This is not your best work, Ms. Ebear had written on my outline. *Please see me after class.*

I wanted to slide down and disappear in my seat when Ms. Ebear handed me back my paper the next morning, but that's hard to do when you are six feet tall. She hadn't even graded it; she'd just written the note.

When World History class finished, I hung back while everyone else left. Ms. Ebear smiled at me, which made me feel awful. She was my favorite teacher, and I had disappointed her.

"Elle, I think you know you could have done better," she began, and I nodded.

"Yes," I replied. I didn't say anything else. My parents had taught me never to make excuses when something had been my own fault. My dad always liked to quote Ben Franklin, who said, "He that is good for making excuses is seldom good for anything else."

"I know you're busy with basketball," Ms. Ebear said, making an excuse for me. "So I'm going to assume that you're adjusting to your new schedule. And since I know you can do better, I'd like to give you a chance to redo the outline. Tonight."

"Tonight?" I repeated. I quickly went over my evening in my head. Practice, Zobe, shower, dinner . . . but I couldn't turn down her offer. "Sure, tonight. I'll hand it in tomorrow."

Ms. Ebear smiled again. "That's the spirit, Elle!" she said. "I'm looking forward to reading your new outline tomorrow."

I thanked her and hurried to Ms. Rashad's science class. She was handing out packets of worksheets to everybody.

"Use these worksheets to help you study for your test tomorrow," she said. "I'm going to give you all some time during class to work on these."

I flipped through my packet. It was four pages of questions about cells, and we could find the answers in our science books. Questions about cytoplasm, ribosomes, lysosomes, mitochondria . . . I realized I didn't know the difference between an organelle and a vacuole and felt a moment of panic. I mean, I had been paying attention in class. Shouldn't I have absorbed some of this stuff?

I got about halfway through the packet when the bell rang, and then, thankfully, it was time for gym. But I was so distracted during volleyball that I sent two crazy serves careening around the gym, and missed an easy ball that Bianca lobbed right at me.

"Don't these teachers know that we have lives?" I complained to Avery at lunchtime.

At lunch I sit with my closest friends on the basketball team: Avery, Hannah, Natalie, Caroline, and Patrice.

"You mean all the homework we've been getting lately?" she asked.

Patrice groaned. "Tell me about it! It's killing me!"

"Yeah, it's like they threw every test and project at us at once," Natalie agreed.

I felt a little bit relieved, knowing my friends felt the same way as I did. I took a bite out of the turkey pita sandwich my mom had packed for me.

"Ebear's project is so much work," Patrice added. "But at least it's interesting."

"And how about those journal entries for English?" I piped up. "I mean, who can write one of those every night?"

Everyone was quiet when I said that, and I had a sinking feeling—a feeling that I was the only one with that problem.

"You mean you do yours every night?" I asked.

"Well, sure," Avery responded. "It's pretty easy."

"Yeah, plus the book is very good," Hannah said.

I lowered my head on the table. "I am doomed!" I said. "I can't keep up with any of this."

Avery patted my shoulder. "You'll be fine, Elle. You can catch up tonight."

"But we have practice!" I said, coming up for air long enough to take a bite of sandwich.

Caroline nodded sympathetically. "It'll be okay, Elle."

"Thanks," I said. I had always been friendly with Caroline, but lately I was wondering how we hadn't become better friends. How I hadn't even known that she had two brothers. It made me want to spend more time with her, but time was not something I had a lot extra of. Especially since I didn't even have time to hang out with Avery, and I barely saw Blake anymore either.

"I just gotta get through practice," I muttered to myself, and then I finished my sandwich.

Because it was Wednesday, I didn't have to worry about Coach Ramirez starting practice with a game tape. We stretched and did laps around the gym, and then we did some shooting drills. I like those way better than footwork drills. One thing I am good at is getting the ball through that hoop.

When practice finished, I promised myself that I would be super focused. I ran around with Zobe in the backyard, showered, and helped Mom with dinner. I wolfed down my food in record time and jumped up, clearing my plate.

"Whoa, Elle, where's the fire?" Dad asked.

"Homework!" I said, and neither of my parents could argue with that. I bounded up the stairs two at a time, with Zobe at my heels. Then I shut the door behind us and got to work.

First order of business was the outline for Ms. Ebear. I spent a whole hour researching so I could add more detail and sources. I looked on the public library's website to find books I could use for the report.

It was eight o'clock when I finished, and I felt good about it. Next I read a chapter in the novel and wrote two journal entries. I still wasn't caught up, but I knew I needed to move on to my science test.

Now it was nearly ten o'clock, and I heard a knock on my door.

"How you doing, Elle?" Dad asked, poking his head into my room. "It's getting late."

"I'm okay," I said. "I just have to study for my science test."

"Fine," he said, "but try to call it quits at eleven, okay?"

"Sure, Dad," I said. "Love you."

"Love you too, Elle!" he said.

I took out my science packet and began searching for answers to the practice questions in my science book. I knew that a nucleus was like the brain of a cell. But what the heck was a golgi body?

"The golgi is a system inside the cytoplasm," I read out loud. "It packages proteins into membranes and ships them to other parts of the cell."

I looked through my notebook. Ms. Rashad had said that the golgi was like the "mail room" of the cell. That I could remember. At least, I hoped I could!

I had a full hour to study for the test. I finished the packet by 10:45, and I knew I should read through it, but I started yawning like crazy. My head started to droop. I woke up with a start at eleven with drool running down my chin. I had fallen asleep over my science book!

I knew there was no point in studying anymore that night. I turned off the light and snuggled in with Zobe. After I fell asleep, I dreamed of a big purple monster named Golgi that wanted to steal my cells and ship them to California.

As it turned out, I would have been better off facing that monster than going to school on Thursday!

Getting It Done!

Explain *the role of mitochondria in cellular respiration.*

I stared at my science test, blinking. I knew that muscle cells have a lot of mitochondria. So I wrote that.

Muscle cells have a lot of mitochondria.

Then I chewed on the end of the pen. Mitochondria . . . muscles . . . mitochondria had something to do with energy, I remembered. But exactly what, I wasn't sure. But I added another sentence.

Mitochondria produce energy for the cell.

That seemed good enough, so I went on to the next question, about the nucleus. For some reason, that's the one I remembered best. The nucleus was like the brain of the cell. I wrote down the answer, hoping that my own brain wouldn't let me down for the rest of the test.

I got through the test without leaving anything blank. But I had a sinking feeling that I was getting a lot of things wrong, or only partly right. When the bell rang, my palms were sweaty and my shoulders were tense.

"Well, that test was pretty rough," I told my friends at lunch time.

"I don't have Rashad until seventh period," Patrice said. "What's on the test?"

"Everything from that packet she handed out," I replied. "So if you studied that, I think you'll be fine. But I ran out of study time last night."

"You're running out of time for a lot of stuff lately," Avery mumbled, not looking at me.

I didn't have to ask what she meant. I knew.

"I'm sorry, Avery," I said. "I know you want to

meet Zobe. It's just . . . everything's been crazy. Between homework and practice and volunteering, I'm just trying to figure it all out. I will invite you over soon, I promise."

"Sure," she said, but she avoided my eyes and dipped her spoon into her yogurt.

I didn't like things being tense with me and Avery. I knew I needed to talk to her more about it, but not in front of everyone in the cafeteria. I'd have to do it soon, though. But when?

It couldn't be after school, because I was volunteering at Camp Cooperation. When the last bell rang at the end of the day, I walked over to the elementary school. Caroline was there when I got there, and Pete ran right up to me.

"Elle, let's go outside!" he said. "Let's play ball!"

Brian approached us. "Are you okay with the outside kids again today, Elle?"

"Sure," I said. "Unless Caroline wants to do it."

"I don't mind staying in," she said, and she grinned. "Besides, Pete would be mad at me if he didn't get to play ball with you."

"You're both good at ball," Pete said. "But I get to play with you all the time, Caroline."

"That is so true," Caroline said, and she rolled her eyes at me. I got the idea that Pete was a little brother who needed a lot of attention.

"Let's go, Elle!" Pete said, and he ran outside. I jogged after him, and Brian followed with Lily, Addie, and Max.

Brian jogged to the edge of the field to grab the soccer ball for Lily and Addie. Pete picked up a rubber ball and ran over to Max.

"Max, let's play quiet ball with Elle!" he said.

Max shook his head.

"Come on Max, let's play!" Pete said.

"I said NO!" Max yelled. Then he took the ball from Pete's hands and threw it right in his face!

I didn't know what to do. Was I supposed to scold Max? Or comfort Pete? Or get between the boys? I froze, because I didn't want to do the wrong thing.

Luckily for me, Pete handled it. "It's okay, Max," he said. He wasn't even mad that Max had hit him with the ball. "I'll get Brian."

Pete ran to get Brian and pointed to Max. Brian hurried over to Max and tossed me the soccer ball.

"Elle, why don't you and Pete kick the ball around with the girls for a bit?" he asked.

"Sure," I said, glad to be told what to do. "Is that okay with you, Pete?"

"Soccer's not as good as baseball, but it's okay," Pete said. I put the ball on the grass in front of him and he started kicking it toward Lily and Addie.

I glanced back at Brian, who was kneeling down and quietly talking to Max. The little boy was nodding calmly. Brian gave him a ball, and for the rest of our time outside he threw it up and caught it, over and over. But he seemed happy.

At snack time, I approached Brian.

"I think I need some training or something," I said. "When Max hit Pete with the ball, I didn't know what to do."

"That's okay," Brian said. "I wasn't far. Still, training's not a bad idea. I'll talk to Janette and Vicky about a volunteer training session."

I looked at Pete, who was eating his apple slices

next to Addie. The two of them were cracking up about something.

"How did Pete know exactly what to do?" I asked.

"Pete and Max have been friends for a few years," Brian replied. "He knows Max really well. And he's also a smart kid."

I nodded. "That's for sure," I said.

I kept thinking about Pete and Max until it was time to go. Pete was a really good friend to Max. He knew exactly what Max wanted. And I knew what Avery wanted—to spend some time with me. I had to make that happen. I promised myself that I wouldn't let anything get in the way of making time for Avery.

Caroline, Pete, and I were waiting to get picked up when Pete said, "Elle, why do you have to go to your house? Can't you come to our house?"

"Sorry, Pete," I said. "But I have to play with my dog and eat dinner with my family. And do my homework."

"Come on Saturday!" he said.

Caroline looked at me and shrugged. "I know

Pete invited you, but I think that would be nice," she said. "If you're free on Saturday."

I searched my mind. I think Avery and I had talked about her meeting Zobe on Saturday. But that wouldn't take all day. I was sure I could do both. And how could I say no to Pete?

"Um, sure," I said. "For a little while. Maybe in the afternoon."

"Yay!" Pete said.

Then my phone beeped with a text from Amanda.

Are we still on for our doggy date Saturday?

Amanda! I'd forgotten all about it. But the doggy date wouldn't take too long—maybe an hour. And Amanda had been bugging me for a doggy date for so long, I hated the idea of disappointing her, too.

Dog park 10 a.m.? I texted back.

👍 she replied.

That made me happy, and I was feeling pretty confident. I was making time for all my friends. Getting my homework done. Volunteering. I was doing all the stuff I wanted to—and needed to.

A little voice inside me asked an annoying question: *But are you doing it well, Elle? Or just doing it?*

I ignored that little voice. I was going to get everything done, and I wasn't going to let anything stop me!

D Is for Disaster

Friday morning started out pretty well. And then it went downhill, fast.

Ms. Ebear handed back my revised outline with an A written on it.

This is the kind of work I expect from you, Elle! she wrote. *Keep it up!*

Seeing that A was a relief, although I knew I still had a lot more to do to finish the project. But it was a good start to being back on track.

My good feeling disappeared in Ms. Rashad's class the next period, when I got my test back. There was a letter I had never seen on a test before: D. My superhero-size confidence vanished in a flash.

"This was the first big test of the year, and a few of you had trouble," Ms. Rashad said. "So I am giving everybody who wants to a chance to retake the test on Monday."

Thank goodness, I thought. If my parents ever found out I had gotten a D on a test . . . I didn't want to think about it. It's not that they would be angry, but I knew they'd be disappointed. And there would be lectures. And maybe some other consequences that I could only guess at.

Then Ethan Ross raised his hand. "Ms. Rashad, are you putting these grades up on the school wires, or waiting until we take the retest?"

"I upload all grades immediately into the system," she replied. "But I will change the grade after the retest."

My stomach sank. I had forgotten all about the school wires. It was a system where parents could log in and check your grades at any time. I knew that

Mom and Dad checked it occasionally. Would they check it over the weekend?

Just tell them, a little voice in my head said. *Tell them and get it over with.*

Maybe, I told the little voice. *Or maybe not. . . .*

I was thinking about that D all day. It hung over my head like a cloud, and that stayed during practice, where I missed three easy shots during shooting drills.

"Elle, watch your form!" Coach Ramirez scolded me. "You're getting sloppy today!"

I saw Bianca smile when Coach said this, but I didn't blame her. I was playing sloppy.

"Is everything okay, Elle?" Avery asked as we waited for our rides in front of the main building.

I hadn't told her about the D on my test yet. I hadn't told anyone.

"Well . . . ," I began.

Before I could say more, Amanda hurried past us to get to her dad's car.

"See you tomorrow, Elle!" she called out with a wave.

Avery raised an eyebrow. "Are you busy tomorrow? I was hoping I could come over and meet Zobe, like we talked about."

"I built in time for you," I said. "I'll be back from the dog park at eleven. Can you come by then?" I asked.

"Mom's taking me shopping," she replied. "I was hoping I could come by in the afternoon."

My brilliant plans to see three friends in one day were rapidly unraveling. I had thought of everything—except to ask Avery when she was free.

I frowned. "I'm . . . I'm doing something," I said. I didn't want to tell her I was going to Caroline's because I knew she'd be jealous. "I'm sorry, Avery."

"It's fine. You're busy," Avery snapped. "We'll do it some other time." And right then, her mom pulled up.

Just before Avery got in the car, Caroline walked past us.

"See you tomorrow, Elle!" she said.

Avery froze. She gave me a look that said, "Are you serious?" Then she got into the car without another word.

"Elle?" Caroline asked. I guess I had been staring at Avery.

"Oh, yeah. Tomorrow. I'll see you then," I said.

Then my mom pulled up. I slid into the passenger seat.

"How was school today?" she asked.

I hesitated. Should I tell her about the D?

Don't tell her unless she asks about the test, another little voice said.

That sounded like a good rule to me.

"Fine," I answered.

"Any plans tomorrow?" she asked.

"I'm taking Zobe back to the dog park in the morning," I said, "to hang out with Amanda's dog, Freckles. They met on a walk and they got along really well."

"That sounds nice, Elle," Mom said. "Are you okay to take Zobe to the dog park, though? I thought you said he needed training."

I had forgotten all about that! "Well, he's good with other dogs," I said. "As long as there are no little kids inside the dog park, we should be fine."

Mom nodded. "That sounds reasonable. Any other plans?"

"Caroline from the team asked if I could come over. Her little brother is Pete, the kid I hang out with at Camp Cooperation," I said. "Can you drive me?"

"I could probably bring you after lunch tomorrow," Mom said. "Would that work?"

"Perfect!" I told her. "Thanks."

That night I was too tired to study, and Dad wanted to watch a movie with me anyway in the living room, so I didn't get any schoolwork done. I didn't think it was a big deal, though, because it was only Friday and I had the whole weekend ahead of me.

The next morning, I met Amanda and Freckles at the dog park. A guy with a German shepherd and a woman with a Boston terrier were there already, but since there were no little kids I felt good about letting Zobe off the leash when we got inside the fence. Amanda did the same with Freckles, and the dog immediately started chasing Zobe.

Zobe let Freckles chase him, and then he stopped and they sniffed each other for a while.

"Good boy, Zobe! That's my good boy!" I praised him, petting his head.

"So, how do you like having a dog?" Amanda asked.

"I love it!" I replied. "He does these sweet, funny things all the time. Like, he puts his head on my lap and his eyes get all big when he wants something. And I like having him sleep with me. Does Freckles sleep in bed with you?"

"Well, I'm not supposed to let her," she replied. "But sometimes I sneak her into my room. I think I sleep better when she's with me, for some reason."

I nodded. "Totally! It's like a stuffed animal, only better."

"And alive," Amanda added with a laugh.

I could have stayed at the dog park all morning. Even though the leaves had all fallen off the trees, it was still beautiful out. The sky was bright blue with white, puffy clouds, and I didn't mind the chilly air. Amanda and I were both wearing our Spring

Meadow winter hoodies, which are lined with fleece and super cozy.

We kept an eye on the dogs as we talked about Mr. Patel, our gym teacher; and the game on Sunday; and our favorite players in the WNBA. We talked about music we both liked (Katy Perry!) and food we both hated (Swiss cheese and bologna).

We didn't talk about the D on my science test, or how I was worried that Avery was mad at me, or anything really important. Part of it was, I didn't know Amanda well enough yet. And part of it was that it was just nice not to have to worry about things for a change.

"Mint chocolate chip is *way* better than rocky road," Amanda was saying (after the conversation turned to ice cream), when I noticed a dad with a little boy approaching the dog park, with a fluffy mutt on a leash. I quickly ran to Zobe and snapped the leash on him.

"Sorry," I said to Amanda. "I've got to take Zobe out. He gets too excited around little kids."

"Oh, sure," she said. "I'll put Freckles on the leash and walk with you."

She whistled to Freckles, who trotted right over to her. Then we made our way out of the dog park and down the path back to the street. We walked for a few blocks and stopped in front of Amanda's yellow house.

"Well, that was a fun doggy date," she said, smiling at me.

"Yeah, really fun," I agreed. "We should do it again sometime."

"I'd like that," Amanda said, and then she quickly added, "and Freckles would too."

I waved and headed to my house, thinking of Amanda's smile the whole way back.

Blake was outside his house when I walked past. He stepped out onto the sidewalk and started talking to me.

"What's for lunch?" he asked.

"How about pb & j?" I asked him.

"Sounds good," he replied.

That was how it was with me and Blake. Living next door to each other made it very easy for us to be friends, and to see each other whenever we wanted. But Avery and I didn't even live in the same town, so it was a lot harder to get together outside of school.

Still, I knew I hadn't been hanging out with Blake as much as usual, so I asked him about it.

"So, I've been, like, pretty busy lately," I said. "Sorry if we're not hanging out enough."

Blake shrugged. "No big deal. You live right next door."

And that was that. Blake and I ate our sandwiches, and after, Mom drove me to Caroline's house. The kids from Spring Meadow lived in all different towns, and Caroline lived in Wilmington, on a tree-lined street with neat brick houses.

When we pulled up into their driveway, the door opened and Caroline came out, along with her mom. Mrs. Lindgren had the same sandy-blond hair and green eyes as Caroline.

As I got out of the car, Mom rolled down her

window. "Hi, Julia. I'll pick up Elle around three. Is that okay?"

"That'll be fine, Jeni," Mrs. Lindgren replied.

As Mom drove off, Pete ran out of the house. "Hi, Elle! Hi, Elle! What are we going to play?"

"Pete, Elle is here to spend time with both you *and* Caroline," Mrs. Lindgren said.

Pete ran into the driveway and picked up a basketball.

"We can all play basketball!" he said. "Right, Caroline?"

Caroline looked at me, and I shrugged.

"Sure," I said.

Pete was already bouncing the ball around the driveway, really high, so it kept getting away from him.

"Pete, bring the ball here!" I told him, and he came running over with it. "I think you need to learn some dribbling drills, okay?"

"Okay," Pete said.

I took the ball from him. I bent slightly forward, keeping my chest and head up. Then I started dribbling the ball with my right arm.

"See how I'm doing that?" I said. "I'm using my whole arm and shoulder when I dribble. It's called pound dribbling. I'm not just slapping it with my hand."

"That's good, Elle!" Pete said.

I passed him the ball. "Now you try."

Caroline had run off, and she came back with a second basketball. She stood next to Pete. "Let's do it, Pete," she said.

Pete dribbled a few times, but the ball kept getting away from him. So I stood behind him and helped him get into the right position. Pretty soon he was pound dribbling like a pro.

"I'm doing it!" he cried.

"Now do a crossover," I said. "Caroline, wanna show him?"

Caroline started to dribble the ball from one hand to the other. Pete had a little more trouble with that.

"I'm tired," he said, and then he dropped the ball, walked over to the lawn, and sat down.

Caroline rolled her eyes. "He gives up so easily

sometimes," she said. "But at least he's outside. Sam stays inside all day playing video games."

I picked up Pete's ball and began to dribble. Then I made a basket.

"Wanna play one-on-one?" Caroline asked.

"Sure," I replied. I put tossed my ball onto the lawn. "You get first shot."

Caroline started dribbling toward the basket. I got in front of her and stole the ball right from her as she was dribbling. Then I turned and sank my shot.

"You stole that from me so easily!" Caroline exclaimed, but she wasn't angry or complaining. She was frustrated.

"Try this," I said, dribbling with my right hand. "Keep the ball in one hand. Then, if a defender comes at you, you can switch hands quickly. Come at me, I'll show you."

Caroline came toward me, and I demonstrated. I dribbled with my right hand, and when she tried to get the ball, I quickly bounced it into my left hand and then turned away from her to make my shot.

"I never knew you could do that!" she said, catching my rebound.

"Jim taught me," I said. "My older brother."

"I wish Coach would teach us useful stuff like this," Caroline said as we continued to play. "And I wish she would let me play more. I bet I could get better if she did."

"I *know* you could!" I said, and I meant it. "You can learn so much by playing in a game. It's the only way to test if you can put what you've learned into practice."

We kept playing our pickup game as Pete cheered us: "Go, Elle!" and "Yay, Caroline!"

"Pete, you're supposed to pick one side," Caroline told him.

"But I want you both to win!" he said.

I won the first game, and we played another. And another. I could see Caroline loosening up and having fun. By the fourth game, she hadn't beaten me, but she was getting closer and closer, and making more shots.

Then Mrs. Lindgren came outside.

"Oh, shoot!" I said. "Is my mom coming soon?"

"That's what I came to tell you," she said. "You looked like you were having fun, so I told your mom that I'll drive you back when you're ready."

"Cool!" I said.

"One more game?" Caroline asked, and of course I had to say yes. I was starting to think that maybe having Jim and Blake to play with my whole life had made me a better, more confident basketball player. This one-on-one time with Caroline seemed to really be helping her. Besides, I was having fun!

Twenty minutes later we were both sweaty and tired and drinking lemonade and eating oatmeal cookies inside Caroline's kitchen with Pete.

"Elle beat you, Caroline," Pete said.

"Yes, I know that, Pete," she said. "She's a very good basketball player."

"And so are you," I said. "I mean it. Coach needs to put you in more."

"Thanks," Caroline said.

"Elle, when are you coming to Camp Cooperation again?" Pete asked. He frowned. "You weren't there on Friday."

"I'll be there on Tuesday," I promised him. "Every Tuesday and Thursday."

"Wow, that's a lot," Caroline remarked. "Between school and basketball and stuff, I can only volunteer one day a week."

"I wish Elle could do every day," Pete said.

"Aw, me too, Pete," I said, but even as I said the words, I wasn't sure if I was telling the truth. I mean, I really liked it. But two days was enough. I totally understood why Caroline volunteered for only one day, but I still felt like I could do two. Like I was really making a difference. And I didn't want to disappoint Pete!

After our snack, Mrs. Lindgren drove me home, and Caroline came along for the ride. (Her brothers stayed home with their dad.) I had fun talking to Caroline, but once again, I got that pang of guilt telling me that I should have been hanging out with Avery instead.

My guilt faded when I got home and the house smelled of Dad's lasagna. As I took my seat around the dinner table, I was thinking about what an awesome day it had been.

And then Mom asked the question I had been dreading.

"Elle, I meant to ask you," she said, "how did you do on your science test?"

I had promised myself I would tell Mom if she asked me directly. I know it was my own rule, and I could have broken it. But once I make a deal with myself, I stick to it.

"I didn't do so great," I admitted. Technically, I was following my rule, and I hoped she wouldn't push it further.

"What grade did you get?" she asked me.

"A D," I said quickly, and then I took a bite of my lasagna.

"Whoa," Jim said, and I kicked him under the table.

"A D," Mom repeated. "And when were you going to tell us this?"

"Well, we're getting a makeup test on Monday, so the D isn't permanent," I explained. "A lot of kids got bad grades. It wasn't just me."

Mom took a deep breath. "I see," she said, and

I knew the wheels in her mind were whirring. "It's good that she's letting you take a makeup test. But I'm guessing you didn't do any studying today."

"Well, no," I said, pushing my food around on my plate with my fork. "I can study tomorrow."

"Yes you can," Mom said. "Before and after your game."

I dropped my fork. "Before? I can't do it before. I have my pregame ritual. You know that!"

"And I respect it," Mom said. "But this test is important. And if you realized that, you would have stayed home today and studied."

"I can study tonight too!" I promised. "It's early."

Then Dad chimed in. Usually he lets Mom take the lead, and then he swoops in at the end to deliver the crushing blow.

"You will definitely study tonight," he said. "And tomorrow morning, and after the game. Your mother's right, Elle."

I felt like crying. The lasagna felt like a rock in my stomach. I got up.

"I'm going to study," I said. I looked at Zobe,

who was patiently waiting for me next to the table. "Come on, Zobe, let's go outside."

I headed out to the backyard with Zobe and tossed him the ball. He was super happy, but I was miserable.

That D was ruining my life. Without my pregame ritual, I knew I wasn't going to play well at tomorrow's game. I was convinced of it.

"I'm going to have bad luck tomorrow, Zobe, I just know it," I told him.

He dropped the ball at my feet and stared at me hopefully, drooling.

Something Lost,
Something Gained

The next morning I woke up at 6:30 a.m., like I usually do now on the morning of a game. I walked Zobe, showered, and ate half a bagel with peanut butter.

But I didn't warm up in our driveway. I didn't nap. Instead, I read about mitochondria and ribosomes.

When it was time to get dressed for the game, I started to put my shorts on—*before* I put on my shoes! The change in my routine had rattled me so much that I was even messing up the stuff that was in my control!

This is going to be a bad game, I told myself.

It wasn't just the change in my morning routine that was worrying me. Today, we were playing the Pine View Patriots. They were the top-rated team in the league.

"I hear that half their team is as tall as Elle!" Patrice had said at Friday's practice.

"I heard their coach makes them drink green juice before every game and they never run out of energy," Hannah had added.

"They beat the Hawks thirty-seven to *nothing*," Natalie added, her eyes wide.

That pressure had been weighing me down too.

Mom and Dad drove me to the Patriots gym. The walls were decorated with so many red-white-and-blue GO PATRIOTS! signs that it looked like wallpaper. They even had cheerleaders! Spring Meadow didn't have basketball cheerleaders at all.

My parents took their places in the stands, and I headed to the court, picked up a ball, and dribbled up to Avery.

"Hey," I said.

"Hey," she said back, but without a smile. I knew she was still mad at me, and I couldn't blame her.

Then Patrice came over and nudged me.

"Did you check out the Patriots over there?" she asked. "Looks like the rumors were true."

I looked over at the opposite side of the court, where the Patriots were already doing their shooting drills. Patrice was right—they were all pretty tall. One of them even looked like she could be my height. They had no really short girls, like most teams had.

"Whoa," I said.

Coach Ramirez came onto the court, clapping her hands. "Okay, Nighthawks! Shooting drills!"

We lined up for shooting drills. Caroline was at the front of my line, and she made her first shot. When she jogged past me, I held out my hand to slap hers.

"Nice!" I said.

"Thanks, *Coach*!" she replied, and I knew she was referencing our basketball session the day before. But the others didn't know that. Avery turned around to raise an eyebrow at me, and then turned right back.

I went through the drill feeling like my head was connected to the rest of my body by a thin string, floating above me like a helium balloon. I made every shot, but that's only because I could do the drill in my sleep.

Then I noticed Hannah's dad, Mr. Chambal. He was pointing his video camera at us as we drilled. It had never really registered before. Lots of parents liked to record the game. But now I remembered that Mr. Chambal's videos were what Coach was using to do her game reviews with. Ugh. I already knew that I wouldn't want to see this game with the Patriots again.

Mr. Chambal's camera watched us as Coach got us together right before game time. Just like last game, Coach started me, Bianca, Avery, Tiff, and Patrice.

I took my place in the center of the court and faced the Patriots center. I realized I was looking right into her eyes, something I wasn't used to. Was this girl really as tall as I was?

Those words were going through my head when the ref's whistle blew. I jumped up—and to my surprise, the Patriots center got to the ball first! She tapped it over my head to a teammate, who started dribbling toward the basket like a streak of lightning.

I was shocked. Coach Ramirez had made me a center because of my height, and now my height didn't even matter! That threw me off big time. If I had felt disconnected from my body during the drill, the feeling only got worse.

I don't remember much about the first half of the game except that the Patriots dominated. Every time I got the ball, one of their defenders stole it from me. I got two rebounds, but didn't score at all. Avery made a couple of shots, and so did Bianca. Tiff scored too. By the end of the second quarter, the score was Patriots 15, Nighthawks 8.

"I know the Patriots are tough," Coach told us. "But you guys have the talent to pull this off. They're intercepting all our passes, so use your feet. Fake going in one direction, and then quickly move in the other. We've got to confuse them."

For the third quarter, she benched me and sent Bianca back in as center and put Tiff in as shooting guard, along with Avery, Caroline, and Dina.

For the first time ever, I felt relieved to be on the bench. I watched as the one of the Patriots players powered down the court and made a failed layup. Caroline was closest to the net and caught the rebound. She started dribbling and I saw her frown. She had Patriots on either side of her. How was she supposed to pull off the fakeout that Coach had suggested?

She didn't. When she couldn't get any farther, she stopped. Then she faked an overhand pass to the left, but quickly turned and lobbed it to Tiff, who caught it. It wasn't exactly what Coach had said to do, but it worked.

Tiff scored from the three-point arc. A few minutes after that, Avery did some fancy footwork and managed to sink a layup. Now the score was Patriots 15, Nighthawks 13.

The Patriots fought back hard. They scored seven points in the next three minutes. Watching them play, I could see why. They were faster than us, and moved more confidently.

That only made me more nervous when Coach called me back in for the fourth quarter.

"You're our best shooter, Elle," Coach said. "I'm counting on you for some points here."

I nodded. "Yes, Coach."

The realization that I had not scored once all game hit me. I don't think I'd ever had a game without scoring, not in my whole basketball career. Not even in third grade. Shooting was what I was best at. Would this be the first game where I didn't score?

As soon as I asked myself that question, I sealed my own fate. I had convinced myself that I would have a bad game the minute Mom told me I had to skip my good-luck routine. And I had made it come true. I had totally psyched myself out!

Here's what happened: Surrounded by defenders at the three-point arc, I took a shot instead of passing, and missed. I got a rebound from Amanda and missed an easy two-pointer. I tried to make a layup, but one of the Patriots got the ball from me as I dribbled toward the basket.

And finally, the unthinkable happened. One of the Patriots jabbed me with an elbow that brought me to my knees. I took a free throw shot—a lousy free throw—and missed!

I couldn't rebound after that—not in any sense of the word. The Patriots scored six more points in the final quarter, and right at the end, Caroline got fouled. She looked calm and focused as she took her shot, and it swished through the net.

"Yay, Caroline! Yay!"

I turned to see Pete in the stands. I'd been so inside my own head for the game that I'd totally tuned out the spectators in the bleachers. It made me happy to see Pete cheering for Caroline, but at the same time, I wished he could have been cheering for me, too. But there was nothing to cheer for.

The buzzer sounded, and the game was over. We'd lost to the Patriots. I didn't even bother looking at the scoreboard. We lined up to slap hands with them.

Right after I slapped the last hand, I could feel the tears forming in my eyes. I had just played my worst game *ever*. I didn't want to face my parents. I didn't want to face my team. So I ran.

I darted to an exit at the end of the gym and ran outside. I leaned back against the school wall, and then I started to cry. Not the movie kind of crying, where glistening tears glide down your face, but the nasty kind, where you're gulping for air and snorting up snot and stuff.

I felt a hand on my elbow and jumped.

"Elle, are you okay?"

It was Avery, and she didn't look mad or annoyed or frustrated. Her brown eyes had that look of concern that I had come to recognize. That look that only best friends can give each other.

"Avery, I am messing up everything!" I blurted, and the words came flowing out like my tears. "I can't keep up with everything that's happening! I can't take care of Zobe, and go to practice and games, and study, and do homework, and volunteer, and spend time with my friends . . . like you!

I want to spend time with you and I can't! And it's not like I like Amanda or Caroline better than you, it's just . . . we have stuff in common, and I want to hang out with everybody, but I don't have time! I just don't have time! But it's not fair, because I want to do everything!"

"Aw, Elle!" Avery said, and she hugged me. "I'm sorry I got salty with you. I could see that you have a lot going on, and I know all of it is important to you. I mean, I should have known. I'm your best friend."

I sniffled and wiped some tears from my cheek. "And I'm *your* best friend."

"Elle, you are an amazing person to try to do everything you do," Avery remarked. "Don't be so tough on yourself. Everyone goes through hard stuff."

"Lately, it seems like I'm the only one *with* stuff," I said. "Remember, a couple of weeks ago you were talking me down from a freak-out at the mall."

I'd had a meltdown while clothes shopping with Avery and Mom to get a dress for the formal dance that the school throws every fall. I hate wearing dresses, especially fancy ones, so the meltdown was not a surprise to anyone. But Avery had gotten me through it.

Avery looked thoughtful for a moment. Then she raised her eyebrows.

"Give me your phone," she said, holding out her palm.

"My phone?" I asked.

"I have an idea, but you have to trust me," she said. "Do you trust me?"

"Of course," I replied. "But my phone's in my bag inside."

"Then let's get it."

Avery and I went back into the gym, where our parents were frantically looking for us.

"Where did you girls get off to?" Mom asked us.

"Don't be mad at Avery," I said. "I ran off, and she followed me."

"You okay?" Mom asked.

I nodded. "I think so," I said. I took my bag from her, got my phone, and handed it to Avery.

"Excellent," she said. "You coming for pizza?"

"No," I replied. "I've got to study."

On the ride home, Dad made the expected comment: "You played your best Elle, and there's no shame in that."

"I'm not so sure I played my best," I admitted. "I think I psyched myself out."

"And that happens to the best of players, Elle," Dad said. "Don't let this one bad game let you doubt yourself. You were born to play basketball."

Born to play basketball. I had never wanted basketball to be my whole life, but at least I'd been having fun at it. I was good at it. Now . . . I wasn't having fun. And I wasn't so sure I was good at it anymore.

The ride home was quiet after that. It was only one o'clock, so I knew I'd have plenty of time to get work done after lunch. It was kind of a relief not to have to worry about running around.

Mom had already made some tuna salad before we went to the game, and I quickly washed up so I could eat. When I came into the kitchen, Beth was sitting at the kitchen table. I went over to her and let her sniff my head. She shook her head in a happy greeting.

Beth knew we had gone to a game, so when we get back I usually sign "happy" to her if we win, or "sad" if we lose. For the first time that season, I signed "sad" into her hand.

Beth signed back to me: *love.*

Beth loved me. She didn't want me to be sad.

"Love," I signed back to her.

And then, like magic, I didn't feel so sad anymore.

My Team of Friends

"A re the Monday blues getting you down? Cheer up! It's pizza day in the cafeterias today!" Principal Lubin announced during homeroom the next morning.

One of the boys in class, Alex, cheered "Yes!" I knew that pizza wouldn't cure *my* Monday blues, though.

At practice after school, I'd have to watch my horrible performance at Sunday's game all over again. And I still had to take my science makeup test.

There were two things keeping me from total despair. One was that I had caught up on all of my homework the day before. I'd studied, finished all of my reading and journal entries, and gotten a lot of work done on my World History project.

The other thing giving me hope was knowing that Avery had some mysterious plan to help me.

"Can I have my phone back now?" I asked her when the announcements were done.

"Not yet," she said. "At lunchtime."

"Why can't you tell me now?" I asked.

Avery shook her head. "'Patience is bitter, but its fruit is sweet.' My mom says that. Actually, some Greek philosopher said it first, but she has a poster of it in her yoga studio."

"Fine. I'll be patient," I said.

I expected the morning to drag on while I waited for Avery to spring her surprise, but instead, it went quickly. Ms. Ebear told us some traditional African myths, and she's a great storyteller so class went quickly. Then I took my science test, and this time, I felt a lot more confident writing the answers. Maybe

I didn't get an A, but I knew for sure that I had got-ten rid of my D.

That confidence boost carried over to gym, where I was back in my volleyball groove, spiking balls over the net like an animal. At one point, Bianca and I were facing each other across the net.

"Too bad you didn't play this good on Saturday, Elle," she said.

"Yeah, too bad," I replied, and then I jumped up to hit the ball across the net. It landed squarely in the middle of the six players on Bianca's team, who all missed it.

"Point!" I yelled, and Blake high-fived me.

So my Monday blues were almost gone by the time I got to the cafeteria for lunch. But I was still extremely curious to find out what Avery had done with my phone. I found her sitting at my table with my phone placed in front of her, next to her lunch bag.

I sat down. "Now?" I asked, reaching for it.

"Wait," Avery said, holding up her hand. "We've got to wait for the others."

She nodded toward the lunch line, where our usual lunch mates were waiting on line for pizza. I was feeling pretty impatient, but I opened my lunch bag and took out the yogurt, banana, and sandwich that Mom had packed for me. Avery smiled at me.

"Please! I can't stand the suspense!" I pleaded.

Then Hannah, Natalie, Caroline, and Patrice walked up with their trays of pizza. Amanda was with them too, which was unusual. She normally sits with her other friends in concert band.

"You guys seriously brought lunch on Pizza Monday?" Caroline asked.

"My mom doesn't believe cafeteria food is healthy. Neither does Avery's," I replied. "What is going on?"

"Okay, fine," Avery said, handing me the phone. "Tap the screen."

I tapped it, and a program popped up: U-Plan. The screen swirled to reveal a calendar for the week.

"U-Plan is the *best* scheduling program," Avery said. "My mom uses it for her yoga studio and she showed me how to use it when school started this year. So I downloaded it onto your phone, and I scheduled your activities for the next four weeks. You can see, it's color-coded. Blue is school. Green is study time. Orange is basketball. Pink is volunteering, purple is Zobe, and yellow is free time."

Speechless, I scrolled through the week ahead. Avery had scheduled out my week to the minute.

"What's this on Saturday at nine a.m.? Zobe training?" I asked.

Avery grinned. "That's the cool thing. I talked to your parents and told them what I was doing, to see if they wanted me to add anything to it. Your dad told me he had just signed Zobe up for obedience training, so he said I could add it to your schedule and surprise you. You and him are going to do it together. But if you have schoolwork to do, he'll take Zobe by himself."

"No way!" I said. That was the best news.

Then I noticed something, and frowned.

"I don't see a lot of pink," I said. "Did you cut down my volunteering?"

"Sort of," Avery replied. "I've got you down for

two Tuesdays every month. Your friends have got you covered for the days you can't go."

"What do you mean?" I asked, confused.

Natalie spoke up. "Well, we all had fun that day we volunteered," she said. "But I didn't think I had time to do it."

"So Avery figured out that we could take turns volunteering one day a month," Hannah chimed in. "And everybody on the team took a day."

"Everybody?" I asked. I glanced over at the table where Bianca sat with Tiff and Dina.

"Everybody," Avery said. "Oh, and Tiff said she'll help you study for your next science test, if you need it."

I felt like crying, but happy tears this time. I hugged Avery.

"This is perfect!" I said. "Thank you so much!"

"It is," Avery said, and her dark eyes twinkled. "I scheduled a time for me to come over and meet Zobe on Saturday."

"Of course!" I said, and then I looked at my friends. "Thank you. You guys are the best."

I was totally amazed that Avery had figured everything out for me, and that all my friends had helped me. I realized I didn't have to be Wonder Woman. That I could ask for help sometimes, instead of trying to do everything by myself.

The best thing about my new schedule was that I could still do other things besides just school and basketball. And I realized that I was glad to see basketball on the schedule. I still wanted to play, even though I'd just had the worst game of my life. And I knew why I felt that way.

I loved the discipline of basketball, and the feeling you get when you make a basket, and the satisfaction of winning. But that wasn't the best thing about playing basketball.

The best thing? All of my teammates. Because when things get tough, and things go wrong, we were always there for each other. On and off the court.

I love my Nighthawks!

Turn the page for a sneak peek at
Out of Bounds.

Reminder: You have basketball practice starting at 3:15, Elle!

The message appeared on my cell phone screen when the last school bell of the day rang. Normally I wouldn't need a reminder to go to basketball practice. There was no way I could forget that I had practice with my seventh-grade team, the Spring Meadow Nighthawks, every Monday, Wednesday, and Friday after school, plus a game every Sunday. Basketball has been my life ever since third grade.

But the reason why my phone *was* reminding me

was because my best friend, Avery, had just downloaded a scheduling program for me. She'd just presented it to me a few hours ago during lunch in the cafeteria. And if it sounds strange that my best friend was scheduling my life for me, there's a pretty good reason.

Recently I almost had a meltdown because of all the things I was busy with: basketball, my new dog, volunteering, homework, helping my family, and hanging with friends. I had been getting bad grades, hurting my friends' feelings, and psyching myself out on the court because I couldn't figure out how to prioritize my time.

Avery's app looked like it was going to fix all that. And I owed my teammates on the Nighthawks a big thanks, too, because they had all offered to take volunteer slots at Camp Cooperation—an after-school program for kids with special needs. I had been volunteering there twice a week, but since my friends were helping out, I could cut down my days to two Tuesdays a month and free up time for the other things in my life.

Today was Monday, and like the app said, I had basketball practice. We practice in the high school gym, which is just a short walk across a field from the middle school. That's because the school I go to, Spring Meadow School, is a small, private school. It's a K–12 school and there are three buildings on our campus: one for kids in K–5, one for kids in grades 6–8, and one for the high school.

I'd been wanting to thank my teammates since Avery had told me the news at lunchtime. As we walked across the field together, I had my chance.

"I want to thank you guys for volunteering at Camp Cooperation," I said.

"I had fun the day we all volunteered as a team," Natalie said. "Those kids are cute."

"Especially your brother Pete, Caroline," Dina remarked.

Caroline's brother Pete is eight years old and has Down syndrome. She and I recently bonded because I have a special needs sister too. But my sister, Beth, is older than I am, and she has different conditions than Pete does.

"He's cute if you only have to spend an hour a week with him," Caroline joked. "But I am really glad that everyone on the team is going to take turns. I know Pete really loves the program—all the kids do."

Walking in front of me were two of our best players, Bianca and Tiff.

"Yeah, Avery told us you needed help organizing your schedule," Bianca said snidely. "Now maybe you can concentrate on your game."

I ignored the comment. Bianca is one of the tallest players on the team, but she's still six inches shorter than I am (I'm six foot). At the start of the season, Coach Ramirez made me center and that really upset Bianca. She's been calling me out ever since.

Tiff is Bianca's best friend, but she's been a little bit nicer.

"I told Avery that I'd help you study for science," Tiff said.

"Yeah, she told me," I replied. "That would be great. Cellular biology is kicking my butt."

Tiff grinned. "Then we will kick its butt together!"

We had reached the high school gym and headed for the locker room. I changed into my practice uniform and laced up my basketball shoes. I'd had to get new ones after my feet literally grew two sizes over the summer, which was probably the only thing I liked about my growth spurt. I am obsessed with basketball shoes and I would buy a new pair every month if I could afford to.

Then I looked in the mirror and pulled my long blond hair into a ponytail. I took a deep breath. Coach Ramirez started each practice with a video review of our last game. Yesterday we'd had a game against the Patriots, and I had choked. For the first time in my entire basketball career, I hadn't scored. I'd even missed a lousy free throw shot—usually my specialty! So I was expecting Coach Ramirez to be extra hard on me.

When we entered the gym, Coach was pacing back and forth in front of the bleachers. On a normal day she looks like she means business, without a strand of her short brown hair out of place, and a

Nighthawks T-shirt that always looks freshly ironed. Today she looked even more serious than ever, her mouth set in a thin line.

"Losing is one thing," she began right off the bat. "Sometimes we lose even though we played our best. But we did *not* play our best."

She hit a button on the keyboard and the game began to play from the start. I was in the middle of the court facing the Patriots center, who was almost six foot tall, maybe an inch shorter than I was. We both jumped up for the ball, and she tipped it before I could.

"You could have had that, Elle!" Coach said. "You're my center. I need you to be hungrier for that ball."

I nodded. I was getting kind of used to Coach singling me out in the reviews by now, so it didn't sting quite as bad. But it still hurt.

Coach's next comment was directed toward Patrice—her daughter, and our starting small forward.

"Patrice, you had a shot there, and you didn't

take it!" she barked. "You need more confidence out there."

Patrice nodded and looked down at her shoes.

How can she be confident when her mom is always pointing out her mistakes? I wondered.

Coach fast-forwarded through the video, stopping in a few places. Some of her comments were general—we needed to be blocking more shots; we had to be careful not to travel with the ball. But I felt like she made comments about me more than anyone else (except maybe Patrice). I just kept hearing, "Elle! You lost focus there." "Elle! That was sloppy footwork." "Elle! You could have taken a shot there."

I glanced over at Avery and she gave me a sympathetic look. She knew that I hated Video Mondays.

Finally we finished the review.

"Everyone on this team has problems traveling," Coach said. "So today we're going to do some control drills."

We had never done control drills before, so I was curious to see what Coach had in mind. First she had us all line up on one side of the court.

"All right, now stand with your right foot forward, in shooting position," she instructed, and we all obeyed. (Natalie, who's left-handed, stood with her left foot forward.)

"Now we're going to play a game of Stop and Go," Coach continued. "When I say 'go,' run forward. When I say 'stop,' stop and return to shooting position."

We did this several times back and forth across the gym. It wasn't always easy to stop with my right foot forward, so I could see why the drill was a good idea. After we did that a few times, Coach changed things up. This time we dribbled while we ran, stopped in shooting position, and then started again. First Coach had us do it slowly, and then faster.

After the control drills, Coach called for a scrimmage.

"Oh great," I said to Avery. "What if I can't score again? Maybe I'm cursed and my scoring days are over."

"Stop psyching yourself out, Elle!" Avery told me. "You're a great shooter and you know it."

Coach divided us up into two teams for the

scrimmage: Me, Avery, Dina, Hannah, and Caroline on one team, and Bianca, Tiff, Amanda, Patrice, and Natalie on the other.

Bianca and I faced each other as center, and when Coach threw the ball up, I jumped as high and hard as I could. I was not going to give Bianca the satisfaction of getting it. Not today.

I tipped the ball to Dina, who pivoted and passed it to Hannah. Hannah dribbled forward a few steps and then stopped and made her shot. It bounced off the rim, but I caught the rebound and sank the ball for two points.

I grinned at Avery. Making the shot was a huge relief! I felt energized, and I had fun with the scrimmage. But Bianca was on fire, too, and her team ended up beating us by two points.

"Great scrimmage!" Coach complimented us as we cooled off from the game. "Now let's go over the Thanksgiving schedule again. Don't forget that we don't have a regular practice on Wednesday, the half day. We'll be meeting outside on the field for a team-building activity. Lunch is on me. Then there's no practice on Friday, and no game on Sunday."

The thought of a break from practice and competition cheered me up—although I was a little afraid of what Coach's idea of a team-building activity would turn out to be. In elementary school, we'd done stuff like make towers out of marshmallows and toothpicks. I couldn't imagine Coach Ramirez doing anything that silly.

We all grabbed our duffel bags from the locker room and made our way through the high school halls to the main entrance, where our parents would come to get us. Just about everyone was talking about their Thanksgiving plans.

"There's a lot of yellow on your U-Plan schedule this weekend," Avery told me. "I hope I can come over and meet Zobe finally."

Zobe is my almost-brand-new dog, a Great Dane my family adopted from the local shelter. Avery had been dying to meet him, but I'd kept putting her off because I was so busy.

"Yes, yes, yes!" I said.

"Great! I'll send you a U-Plan request, and if

you approve, it will automatically upload into your schedule," she said.

"I have no idea what you just said, but it sounds good," I replied.

Amanda, who'd just started playing basketball this year, chimed in. "I would love to go on another doggy date with Freckles and Zobe, but we're going to my grandmother's this weekend in Pennsylvania."

Freckles is an English springer spaniel with cute freckles, just like Amanda. I was just starting to get to know Amanda, and we'd had some great walks and talks in the park with our dogs.

"Is Freckles going with you, or do you have to put her in a kennel?" I asked.

"Grandma loves dogs, so Freckles is allowed to come with us," she replied.

"That's nice," I said. "We've got our family coming over this Thanksgiving, so we don't have to travel anywhere. I wonder how Zobe's going to be with a lot of people in the house, though. He's a pretty good dog, but we haven't started his obedience training classes yet."

"He'll be fine," Amanda assured me with a smile. "He's a big sweetheart."

Bianca, Tiffany, and Dina were walking behind us, talking with one another, and right at that moment, Bianca's voice got really loud.

"It's about time Coach let me play center already," she was saying.

Normally I would have ignored her. And I might not have argued with her, because I had been a shooting guard in the past and hadn't even wanted to be center when Coach gave me the position. But now I was the center, whether I liked it or not, and I was tired of Bianca giving me a hard time about it.

I turned around. "Bianca, can't you just give me a chance, please?" I asked. "The season just started, and the pressure you're giving me just isn't helping."

Bianca rolled her eyes. "If you can't take the pressure, Elle, then you shouldn't be center," she said. "That's the whole point. It's all about pressure."

Then the three of them walked past us.

Avery shook her head. "I do not understand what her problem is."

"I think she really loves the game more than any-thing," Natalie said. "That's why she works so hard, and why she cares about how everybody else on the team is performing."

"Good point," Hannah said. "I'm glad she's on our team, and not on anybody else's."

I didn't chime in. I was replaying Natalie's words in my head.

She really loves this game more than anything.

That was sure true about Bianca. But was it true about me? Did I love basketball more than *anything*?

And if I didn't . . . well, what did that mean?

Looking for another great book?
Find it
IN THE MIDDLE.

Fun, fantastic books for kids
in the in-be**TWEEN** age.

IntheMiddleBooks.com

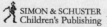 SIMON & SCHUSTER
Children's Publishing   **f** /SimonKids   🐦 @SimonKids

From World Cup Champion and Olympic Gold Medalist

ALEX MORGAN

comes an empowering series about soccer,
friendship, and working as a team.
Join Devin and the Kicks as they chase their
championship dreams.

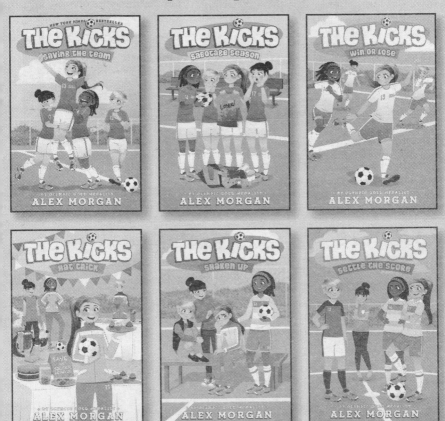

PRINT AND EBOOK EDITIONS AVAILABLE
From Simon & Schuster Books for Young Readers
simonandschuster.com/kids

From the critically acclaimed author of *Amina's Voice* comes a slam dunk new chapter book series about a scrawny fourth grader with big-time hoop dreams . . . if he can just get on the court.

Zayd Saleem, Chasing the Dream!

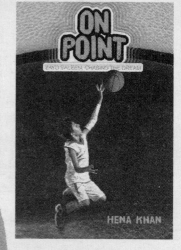

"*Readers will cheer for Zayd.*"
—*Kirkus Reviews* on *Power Forward*

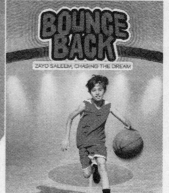

PRINT AND EBOOK EDITIONS AVAILABLE

SALAAM
READS

simonandschuster.com/kids